TWENTY YEARS GONE

LONESOME IN THE HEART OF TEXAS

A. AINSWORTH

1

If you ever need evidence of how Jesus can change someone's life, consider mine. My choices for forty years were sideways on my better days. If there was a poor decision to make, you can bet I made it. But then I met Jesus, and He has been redeeming my past ever since.

I remember a mostly one-sided conversation I had with Coach Flaherty, my middle school football coach, during the fall of my eighth-grade year. He glared across his ancient metal desk in the cramped laundry room that doubled as a coach's office and training room. Then, his demeanor softened as he spoke with the tone of a parent, more concerned with my direction as a young man than with my ability to help his football team win games. He lost me with the first word out of his mouth.

"Braden, if you quit this team today, you'll be preparing yourself to quit more important things in the future. When circumstances at work don't go your way, you'll quit. When you and your wife disagree about some aspect of marriage one day, you'll quit. And if you have kids, you will face adversity there, too. Some parents hang in there and others don't. You're laying the groundwork to quit that, too."

Coach Flaherty's words were those of a prophet that afternoon so long ago. I couldn't imagine him being right because I hadn't slept the previous night for hammering out the speech I had delivered before he hammered out his vision of my future. He nailed it, though. I have quit more jobs than I can count, run out on my wife and kids, walked away from friendships, and the list goes on. If you could be a professional quitter, that's what would lead my resumé. Had Coach pronounced my name correctly—it's *Brandon*, not *Braden* —I was still impressionable enough that I might have listened. I wish I would have taken heed to his words, anyway. As it was, I walked the halls of my school with my chest poked out, bragging about how I told Coach off and how I quit. The team wasn't winning any games that year, so he became an easy scapegoat for my sorry attitude.

I have tried for years to recall what stirred me up to quit, but I can't. Must have been something important. The other quits came in rapid order after that, starting with Boy Scouts. To know me later, you would have never guessed that I was fast tracking toward Eagle Scout at one point. Most of my friends came from football and Scouts, so I guess you'd say I quit them, too.

From then until Jesus saved me in my late thirties, I bounced from friend group to friend group.

My preppy high school friends talked me into going to Ole Miss with them, and I had a blast. Pledging a fraternity was fun, especially since going to class wasn't part of my routine. I told my parents I had a two-five grade point average and made plans to return to school second semester. What I didn't explain was my actual 0.25 GPA. A week before I was to head back to school, my mom was cleaning my room and found my grades. She hit the roof, and I hit the road to whoever would allow me to crash on their couch. Problem was, most of my friends were days away from heading back to college. If I had any sense about me, I would have apologized to my parents and taken what I had coming to me. But my pride wouldn't allow my better sense to choose that route. Plus, they were in their forties when Mom gave birth to me, so I didn't figure they could relate to my struggles. My relationship with my parents was never the same after that, and they died before I could patch up the hurt I caused.

With my frat boy friends gone, I found a new set of companions in the guys from my high school who had gone to trade school or taken a blue-collar job. As I continued to couch surf, I added job surfing to my resume. I worked as a gopher on a construction crew for a year-and-a-half, made good money for my age, dressed in work boots and blue jeans, and bought a truck. I could have kept my head down and nose clean and learned to do something that would have paid me a decent wage. Instead, when I messed up the boss's lunch order one day and he told me to go back and make it right, I informed him what he could do with his lunch. Yeah, I wasn't the sharpest tool in the shed.

I missed a truck payment and figured I'd better find another job if I wanted to keep it. Christmas was coming up, so I picked up some work delivering small appliances in my truck. That was nice money… for a month, but my income fell off a cliff after the holiday delivery season. Two, three jobs later, I needed a change. Each job I worked impeded on what I desired for my life at that point: to not work. I decided to quit my latest job as soon as I made the last payment on my truck and hang out for a while to discover myself. I had buddied up with a dude named Jimmy, who owned a little bar next to the industrial district, and crashed in his basement. What money I had left I spent at his bar.

Just when a repair I couldn't afford effectively took my truck, my great-aunt died. I don't remember ever meeting her, but she left behind a hatchback nobody in the family wanted. My parents had little to do with me by then, but they knew I didn't have a ride, so they gave me the car. They meant it as a jab, and I recognized it, but it was a chance for me to get a free car, so I took it. I was slumming and looked the part, but I'd tell people I was thinking of joining the Peace Corps. They bought it, especially the girls at the bar.

Not two weeks after I inherited the hatchback, Jimmy informed me his wife wanted me out of his house. I squeezed out another six weeks at his place with the promise of a job, but the best I could come up with was hustling pool at Jimmy's Place, not exactly a full-time income. It was just me and Ol' Betty then, with an occasional shower at Jimmy's house when his wife was at work. When I figured I was out of options, I thought about joining the army, but that wouldn't have ended well. That's when I locked eyes with a cute, slightly drunk brunette at Jimmy's bar.

PAULA and I clicked right away because, like me, she was a runaway of sorts. But who am I kidding? She was the runner. I was the quitter. Our common trait was a desperation to fit into a world into which we didn't fit. Have you ever noticed that the loners end up finding each other? It's the same with creatives and rejects and druggies and so forth. Perhaps it's the part deep of our soul that craves community, even if our outer selves reject the notion. Despite our best efforts to live free of the expectations of others, we end up talking and acting much like others with whom we choose to associate.

Pardon me for waxing poetic from time to time. Paula brought that out in me. The first night we met at Jimmy's Place, we talked crazy like that. She wanted to impress an older, intellectual type like me, or at least the me I was pretending to be during that phase of finding myself. I wanted a place to sleep for the night, no matter how deep into it I needed to talk. I slept on her couch that night, but pretty soon I was shacking up at her house most of the time.

Paula was everything I wanted in a girlfriend—good looking, employed, and willing to buy my sob story. She also turned out to be what I needed in a woman, but I wasn't ready for that level of commitment. Oh, I thought I was from time to time with the right mixture of booze, stimulating conversations about dreams I would never fulfill, and physical interaction. A few times I considered marrying Paula, and one time I did it out loud.

The next thing I know, I'm headed to the coast with a new wife in the passenger's seat. Paula had finagled me a job driving a forklift for the trucking outfit where she worked, and we were rolling in more money than I had ever known. I wanted to take her to the casino and live it up for our honeymoon, so I took a grand from the bank account to which she had been so gullible to add my name. Here I was driving my new wife's car, ready to spend her money she had saved from having a stable job longer than I had ever held one. Perhaps another man in my position would have realized how fortunate he was and made some lifestyle adjustments. Me—I shot it all to Hades by sundown.

As responsible as Paula seemed to be, I naturally assumed she was twenty-one, twenty-two, a year or two younger than I was. Turns out she was only eighteen. She claims her age never came up in any of our discussions. I accused her of holding out on me, like I was this trophy husband she didn't dare lose or something. When she informed me she couldn't go into the casino with me because she was too young, I took a figurative pistol and shot myself in the foot. She had every right to go back home right then, annul our marriage, and send me packing forever. That's what I would have done if I were in her shoes. She would have, too, if she had understood annulment.

But then I won several thousand dollars at the casino and made my new wife promises I never intended to keep. One thing I could say I admired about Paula in those days was her relentless optimism. She never saw a problem without seeing an opportunity. With a guy like me—the guy that I was—that can cost you. It cost Paula years of misery as I spent our winnings and our earnings on a truck and a bass boat. What I gave her in return were empty promises of a trip to the beach, where she dreamed of going.

The more time I spent with my fishing buddies, the more we talked about leaving our "old ladies" and enjoying some real freedom. Our Saturdays on the lake were free from the hassle of nagging wives and housework. One guy felt a twinge of guilt for all the time we were spending away from home and suggested we invite the girls one weekend. Since I had used the ruse of Paula and me spending more time together to buy my boat in the first place, I figured it wouldn't hurt to take her once.

To say we took our wives and girlfriends to the lake would be disingenuous. We dropped them off under a tree with plenty of shade and lit out to fish for an hour... or so we told them. We stayed out until we ran out of beer and wanted a bite to eat. Paula had packed a nice picnic basket, but I dared not risk my man card by complimenting her on it in front of the others. Instead, when she pulled a bottle of sparkling grape juice out of the basket, I humiliated her by saying something stupid about her age. She sulked about it, but I held firm and ate my lunch before driving her home. I can't say that I blamed her, but I wasn't about to admit it. As the days passed without our talking it out, I somehow convinced myself that she was in the wrong, and I considered leaving her.

I know. I'm not a very likable person. At least I wasn't then. But the rabbit hole of my narcissism hadn't yet reached its ultimate and predictable dead end.

When I walked in from Jimmy's Place one night later that week, Paula had cooked supper, which she hardly ever did. She used our nicest dishes and glasses, even lit some candles I didn't know we had. That's the night she informed me I was going to be a daddy. If ever a life event was going to turn my selfish rear end around, this was it. And it did… for a few hours. I even suggested we go to church together the following morning, though Paula took it as more of a promise than an honorable intention. By Sunday morning, the excitement of the having a baby gave way to the responsibility that loomed less than nine months away.

By now, you know I didn't handle that well.

2

My daughter's birth kept me around for a while longer, but Paula and I fought all the time. I took out my frustrations with her on a pitcher of beer at Jimmy's more and more often. Making up was fun, but I had checked out as a dad and husband. Paula did nothing wrong, but I still felt compelled to run. I confess I abandoned her to raise our daughter, even earned myself a DUI half a mile from home. At the same time I was drifting from Paula, I was trying my dead-level best to get fired from my job on the docks. I used sick days to sleep in and to go fishing until they expired. Paula was working just as hard on me and our boss to keep me employed until I woke up and manned up.

One night at Jimmy's, I met a guy who offered me an escape. Larry Stearns was in town from Richardson, Texas, for his grandmother's funeral, and we struck up a conversation over a beer and then two and then three.

When I expressed a desire to get away from Harriston and start over somewhere else, he hinted about a distribution network he had begun that might offer me an opportunity in Texas. The work wasn't difficult, he claimed, and the pay beat any other job I would find. He gave me his number and told me to call if I made the move.

I was giving it some serious consideration on the drive home that night. When I walked in the door, Paula was lighting candles. Oh, great, I thought, she's pregnant again. Only, I didn't just think it. I said it. If I was feeling squeezed before, that was the tipping point. I called Larry the next day and strategized my exit plan. I crashed at a friend's house one night as a test run before I left for good. By then I had more or less emptied our bank account. I sold my boat to one of my fishing buddies, loaded my truck, and drove west with no intentions of ever coming back.

I FELT little guilt about leaving Paula the way I did. I keep trying to tell you I was worthless. On my way out of town, I called Larry Stearns and informed him I was en route. He gave me his address, told me to park around back, and welcomed me to stay with him and his wife for a few days. I wasn't there for thirty minutes when he lit a marijuana joint and handed it to me. That was my introduction to Larry's so-called distribution network. I didn't go to Texas to deal drugs, but the money was quick and easy, and the time off was more in line with my motivation. A few days at Larry's house turned into weeks and then months.

One morning, I woke up earlier than usual—before noon—and decided to cook some breakfast. When I reached for the doorknob of my room, I heard Larry and his wife rattling around down the hall from my room. The unmistakable sound of a spring and some sort of door shutting caught my attention before I opened my door. When it came to dealing drugs, I was a small fish since I was new in town and hadn't made many connections. However, Larry's operation was more vast than I could have imagined based on his dump of a house. I normally came in around two in the morning with my take, and he would stuff it in a cash box that couldn't have held more than a few thousand dollars. With other "sales associates" coming and going at all hours of the night, I suspected a cache somewhere in the house. Larry and Bertice never left me alone in the house to search for it.

As much as the Stearns didn't trust me, I felt the same about them. I had my boat money and the cash Larry had paid me stuffed in various places in my duffel bag. It amounted to close to seven grand, and they could have wiped me out anytime they wanted. I searched for a cheap place close by but off the grid and found one several blocks away. When I stopped in the apartment office and asked about a cash discount, the girl behind the desk didn't bat an eye. I paid a deposit and waited until the first of the month for the next available apartment. At that point, I had been staying with the Stearnses for six months. Bertice had been eager to evict me for the last four. I didn't want to invite an opportunity for them to search my bag when I was out and take what they wanted, so I didn't tell them about my new place.

About a week before I would have moved, another small-time operator in the Stearns network sold some pills to an undercover police officer. Jones—not his real name—was a good guy, not your typical drug dealer, for sure. We had stopped in for a beer late one night before we took our till back to Stearns, and he told me the story of his wife's cancer. I was dealing drugs because I was lazy and unmotivated to earn an honest living, but he had just taken a job as a shop supervisor at a cabinet-making plant. It was a good-paying job, but his insurance hadn't kicked in when his wife's doctor diagnosed her with leukemia. The insurance company wouldn't cover her treatment during his ninety-day probation period. This guy was desperate, reaching out to the lowlife drug dealer he was about to fire from his company for a connection to a lucrative part-time career. I felt so sorry for the guy that I gave him a thousand bucks money the next day, no strings attached, as a sort of penance for the seedy life I had chosen. He told me if he could ever pay it back, he would.

His time to make good on his promise came two days later when the police arrested him and took him back to the local precinct to interrogate him. He slipped away to the bathroom, where he texted me that he had been arrested and charged with possession with intent to sell. Jones had told me two nights earlier that he would give up Stearns before he would leave his wife to face her treatments alone. As soon as I read his text, I told Larry and Bertice I needed to go to the laundromat. That wasn't unusual because I washed clothes and met clients there. Only this time, I stuffed every dollar I had into my laundry bag. I hoped to be gone when and if the police came calling at the Stearns' house, but I wasn't taking any chances. I rented a storage unit, where I stored one worn-out pair of boots stuffed with seven thousand dollars in cash.

When the police showed up the next morning, they found me asleep on the couch, my duffel bag on the floor beside me. It contained nothing incriminating, but they arrested me along with Larry and Bertice when they found a stash of drugs and two thousand dollars in cash in their bedroom. The police charged all three of us with possession with intent to sell and a plethora of other charges. From my arrest to my meeting with the court-appointed defense attorney to my testimony before the judge, I claimed ignorance. I told the truth about meeting Larry Stearns in Harriston and crashing at his house when I moved to Texas. Though I may have fudged a bit about how long I had been staying with them, the judge bought it. When I produced a receipt for a deposit on my apartment and assured the judge would never see me in his courtroom again, he dropped the charges against me. The glare in his eyes when he turned me loose guaranteed he expected me to keep my word.

Larry and Bertice didn't fare so well. They judge

sentenced them to seven years apiece because the Stearnses had skirted the law until then. I waited a week and cased their house. The cops had surveilled it for three days, but the coast was clear. I tiptoed through the back alley and onto the back porch. Larry had slipped up and pulled the spare key from under a flowerpot one day after we had gone to the grocery store together and Bertice wasn't answering the door. I found the key right where he returned it and entered like I owned the place.

From my former room, I retraced in my mind the direction from which the noise from the spring had come. Ten minutes later, under a pile of blankets in the hall closet, I found the trapdoor. Inside, I removed two boxes, a shoebox containing a variety of pills and a copy paper box filled to the top with stacks of money. I returned the smaller box to its compartment and walked away with the cash, being careful to leave everything else as I found it, right down to the key under the flowerpot.

I was as nervous as a cat walking down that back alley to where I had parked my truck. I had no story for why I was carrying a box full of money down a back alley at two o'clock in the morning. My whole body shook when I walked into my second-floor apartment, locked and bolted the door behind me, and dumped the box onto my bed. I counted until daylight—seventy thousand dollars. Was I really going to swipe drug money? The list of who stole it couldn't be long, and Stearns seemed the type to send a heavy to collect. On the other hand, he had avoided the law for so long because he had kept his mouth shut. He seemed the type to wait out his seven years and pick up where he left off, starting with the money no longer hidden in his closet. I would be long gone by the time he returned for it. A week after pilfering the cash, I came back for the drugs to replenish my supply. When it ran out, I retired from the drug business… for the first time.

I POSSESSED A FAIRLY unique characteristic among drug dealers when I was in the business: I didn't use. Other than an occasional toke on a joint when expected among other dealers, I despised the stuff. My perpetual haze was brought on by a self-inflicted desire to avoid responsibility. With seventy thousand dollars, minus my first prepaid two months' rent and a sturdy safe, I could live my dream. A year of watching TV most of the day gave way to reading books I had avoided in school and going out to the movies once or twice a week.

My other foray into public life was securing my spot at the bar at Jernigan's Bar & Grill on Sixth Avenue, which was walking distance from my apartment. I befriended the barkeeps and some of the other regulars. Besides my monthly trek to the office of my apartment complex to pay my rent, this made up most of my social interaction for my first five years in Richardson, Texas. On occasion, I ran across one of my former clients who wondered what had happened to me. I told them I gave up the business when the police busted Stearns. No product, nothing to sell.

Four years into my self-indulgent routine, I was

hustling pool at Jernigan's when Jones walked through the door alone. I hadn't communicated with him other than a quick text to thank him for the heads up on the potential Stearns bust. I recognized him right away and wondered if I should approach him at his table near the back. His eyes flitted between the door and the bar like he was looking for someone. Halfway through his first beer, he stood and walked to the bathroom by the pool table where I was playing. I locked eyes with him on his way past. He said nothing, but I caught a glimmer of recognition. On his way back to his table and without looking at me, Jones mumbled, "Give it a minute and join me."

"You shouldn't leave your drink unattended," I offered, slipping into the booth opposite a snitch. "Here, let me order you another one."

He held up his hand to stop me from drawing attention to our table. "No need. I won't drink any more of it. Can't stand the taste of the stuff."

"Why would you come to a bar and order one?"

"I wanted to find you, see how you were getting along after… you know."

"Jones, you don't look so good. Is somebody threatening you?"

"No, at least not yet. I'm thinking about moving my family away from here before the Stearnses get out."

"That's three years away. You act as though they're around the corner and coming for you."

"You think it's three years. What if they get paroled? I'm scared because I ratted them out. You should be concerned because you had more access to than anybody else. Don't you imagine they will come out pointing the finger at one or both of us?"

"Unless they've rehabilitated," I offered without conviction. Jones's question shook me, but I tried not to let it show. "I'm sorry if this is a touchy subject, but your wife..."

"In remission. If she hadn't gotten the care she needed early on, her doctor told us it might have been a different story. I can't thank you enough, Brandon... if that's your real name."

"Yeah, Brandon Gull, the bird from the beach."

"Mine's Jonas Jackson."

"Didn't think it was Jones."

"Close enough. I didn't plan on dealing drugs long, so it didn't need to follow me to my real life. The dealer at my work who pointed me toward Stearns already mispronounced my name as *Jones,* so I went with it into my undercover world. Call it a bridge policy until we could get my wife on my insurance at work, which human resources did for us after ninety days."

"Glad to hear that. I've wondered about her. I considered texting you a few times, but I didn't in case... you know."

"I appreciate the thoughts. That was a strange time in my life that I'd just as soon leave behind forever. My wife doesn't know the nature of the extra work I picked up to pay her medical bills. You're the only one I told both sides of my story. I needed to see you one more time to close the books and thank you again for listening to me. It kept me from going crazy living my double life." He slid a thick envelope across the table. "It's all there, plus interest. Thank you, Brandon."

"Jones—um, Jonas—I never expected to see this again. That money was a gift." I almost added that it was the one unselfish act I could point to in a life filled with quite the opposite. Accepting his repayment would negate my occasional hope of being anything better than what I was. I accepted it, though, because I understood his need to put me in his past along with the rest of his brief but sordid trek into the underworld. Jonas Jackson was as fine a person as I had hopes of knowing. Deep in my soul, I understood that when he walked out the door, I would never see him again.

I threw out an innocuous question to keep him at the table. "How did you find me?"

"I remembered you liked to hang out at night before and after your 'shift,' so to speak, and drink beer. One time when I was driving home from one of my son's baseball games over this way, I noticed you getting out of your truck and walking inside the pub here. I found a reason to drive by on other occasions, but I never saw your truck again. I thought about stopping in and asking about you, but what would I say if they asked me how I knew you? Plus, I wasn't sure Brandon was even your real name."

"If you wanted to find me, you lucked out seeing me at my truck. I almost never drive it here since my apartment is within walking distance."

"Anyway, I'm glad I found you. Listen, I need to get going."

"Are you still working at that same cabinet factory?"

"No, I left there when Jenna's leukemia went into remission. I said you were the only one I told about my brief side hustle, but you weren't the only one who knew. Remember, I told you about the lowlife that I was about to fire who introduced me to Stearns? Well, he kind of had me over a barrel. I told the higher ups I felt like I could help him out, that he reminded me of a younger version of myself. An old boss impacted my life, so I could act as a mentor to him. It was bunk, but I couldn't have him revealing my secret, or I'd be out the door with him. I stretched it out for two years before finding a better job an hour east of here. I resigned my position days before they would have forced my to fire him."

"Dang, man, you always seem to escape trouble in the nick of time."

"Touché."

"I could use some of that."

"Hey, you could be locked right now."

"You're right."

"Brandon, it's been nice talking to you, but…"

"Jonas, if I tell you something important, do you promise to keep it a secret?"

I was not behaving like the clean break from his past that Jonas came looking for at Jernigan's. He broke nervous, but the weight of the source of my carefree life-style pounced on me with a vengeance after hearing of my cohort's exit from the life of crime we had shared. The life I was still profiting from four years later.

"O-kay, sure." He was uncertain he wanted to hear my story.

After being careful no one else was close enough to overhear, I leaned across the table and confessed, "The Stearns left a box full of money under a trap door. The police never found it."

3

Jonas whistled and leaned back in his seat. After another glance around to make sure no one overheard, he leaned forward and whispered between clenched teeth, "How much have you spent?"

"Too much."

"For real, how much?"

"Toward the bottom of the box."

In that moment Jonas saw me for who I was and not the guy who gave him money for his sick wife. "You mean to tell me you've been living off that money for *four* years?"

I would love to say having to answer that question marked rock bottom for me. It felt like it at the moment.

"What's your plan?"

"Get the hell out of here before Larry Stearns or his hitman comes searching for me."

"Why haven't you already done that?"

"I don't know." The fact is that I understood very

well that my lack of ambition kept me in a mindless routine, dulled by a false sense of security. The money was running out faster than my ability to concoct a plan to avoid confronting Larry Stearns.

"I showed up tonight to put this episode of my life behind me for good. You did me a solid back then, but I'm not sinking back into the underworld."

His abrupt tone hammered home the shame I felt in exposing myself to him. "I'm not asking for anything, Jonas. I don't even know why I told you. You just seem like someone I can trust."

"Brandon, if your life is in danger, I would do my best to help you out, but how would I explain that to my wife and kids. They have no idea…"

"Look me in the eye." His eyes darted around the room, scared someone was waiting to hurl his life back to its most regretful place. He forced himself to fix his eyes on mine at me. "Jonas, no matter how much you say you owe me, I never expected you to pay me a dime. I'm not sure why I told you what I did tonight, but I wish I would've let you go back to your regular-guy life. Jonas, I'm happy for you. I guess I needed to tell somebody, confess it. I don't want to drag you into my problems, so when you walk out of here, please don't look back. Delete my number from your phone."

"I wouldn't do that. But, geez, Brandon, you've got to move. Start a new life, man." He stood to leave but hesitated when he stepped toward my side of the booth. "Let me know if I can help." Fifteen seconds later, he was out the door.

He said it because he was that kind of guy, not from

genuine concern, but he would answer if I called. In that moment, I believed I would never face the danger he feared. I didn't count his money until I reached my apartment later. Two thousand dollars in crisp hundreds, double what I had given him. With that and the seven grand that was mine when I left the Stearns, I could make a new start somewhere else.

What direction could I turn, though? Here I was, a career freeloader, with no skills besides shooting pool, which brought in a few thousand before the regulars at Jernigan's learned to avoid me. In the weeks after my visit with Jonas Jackson, I concocted several plans to move off and start a new life.

All of my escape strategies contained varying degrees of hilarity. I started with the ones that took scant effort to create but more effort than I was willing to expend to execute. I would move to Mexico or some Caribbean island and sip margaritas on the beach. That would require a passport I didn't possess. I could roam the country staying in cheap motels and hustling pool from town to town. After a few scrapes with local sore losers, I had no desire for that life. As a passing fancy, I considered going back to Harriston and claiming I had turned over a new leaf. I had burned my parents too many times, though, and we hadn't spoken in years. They might not buy a "new me," even if it was genuine.

I thought about Paula often. I hadn't looked at women the same after leaving her. Somewhere in the recesses of self-absorption, I never wanted to bail on another woman like I did Paula. Sometimes in my half-lucid moments before waking in the mornings, my latest strategy for a clean break from Richardson, Texas, involved her and my kids. My kids. What a joke. After Lisa almost moved me into responsible adulthood, they were growing up without me. My son—I wasn't even sure Paula had named him David like we had decided—was growing up without a father. Somehow, I would one day say I'm sorry to the three of them if they would give me the time of day to say it.

In all my scheming, one nagging thought persisted: it was time for Brandon Gull to grow up and become a productive member of society. With my lack of skills, every road was a dead end. I didn't consider college since it was an unmitigated disaster the first time. Trade school? That sounded like the best choice. I looked into driving a truck, welding, even cutting hair, but the cost was most of what I had left. Construction was booming in Texas and many other parts of the country, so I figured that might be an easier path to decent money. However, the idea of fifty and sixty hours a week of hard labor put that idea on the back burner.

The most sensible route was to join the military. I could bring in a decent paycheck and put money away to start over again. They would teach me a skill to make a living at the end of my stint. Another plus for the military was the housing benefit—that of being far away from Larry and Bertice Stearns when they came searching for their money and the man who stole it.

I could have started over doing any of the jobs on my list, even if I needed to spend the rest of my money picking up the requisite skills. I mulled over my decision for days that became weeks and then months.

When the Stearns money ran out and I started using my own, I drove a mental stake in the ground, setting April 30 as my drop dead date to choose my new direction. That was three weeks away. I felt a surge of adrenaline when I wrote it down and a sense of taking responsibility for my life when I picked up an application from a construction company that was hiring. They told me I would have to pass a drug test and be willing to work out of town during the week. No problem there.

I spent the three weeks before my day of reckoning much like I had spent the previous five years, only instead of watching TV or reading a book, I mapped out my future. I enjoyed writing in a notebook the possibilities for advancement that the eager office manager had pointed me toward when she gave me the application. At night I went to the movies and shot pool at Jernigan's. Though I didn't inform the regulars at the bar about my upcoming career path change, I approached the night of April 29 as a last hoorah of sorts. I informed them I would be spending the next little while on the road. Working. Staying at a hotel. Going to bed early. Repeating the cycle all week. Coming home to rest on the weekends. Earning a paycheck. Starting a new life.

At nine o'clock on the nose, Larry Stearns walked through the door of Jernigan's Bar & Grill, marched to where I was shooting pool, and opened a conversation with a right cross to my jaw.

When I forced my crumpled body off the floor, having taken the shot I deserved, I flailed in desperation at Stearns. I missed and fell to the hardwood again, willing my forearms in front of my face in case he came at me when I was down. I would have deserved that, too, because I had figuratively done that to him. Instead, he stood over me shouting, "Where's my money!" amidst his expletive-filled demonstration. His groin was perfectly positioned for a cheap shot, but I waited for help instead.

Jernigan's didn't employ a bouncer, per se. However, the bartenders made it well known among the regulars that a group effort to remove troublemakers would be rewarded with liquid bonuses commensurate with the level of any commotion. Had the half dozen heavies who came to my aid been aware of why Stearns was attacking one of their own, they would have waited longer. As it was, they stepped in before he launched in again. Had he given in to their admonitions to remove himself from the bar, we might have worked out our differences with no damage other than the trickle of blood on my cheek where his ring had caught me. Stearns didn't budge, though, instead continuing to demand his money.

I was careful not to answer in case the altercation escalated. It did. As the toe of his boot connected with my ribcage, the bartender called the police, who arrived amidst another flurry of requests for repayment. Stearns was more than willing to point the finger at me as the source of the melee, but every other finger in the bar pointed in his direction. Still, the responding officers carted us both off to jail, figuring the judge could make more sense of the situation.

Stearns and I found ourselves in a fix of opposite sorts. He had his wife he could phone, but she had no money with which to bail him out, and I had money but no one to call. Except Jonas Jackson. I hated to ask him to entangle himself in a fight between Stearns and me, but he said if I found myself in peril, to reach out to him. And I needed help. I dared not call him by name after he answered my call, nor mention my antagonist, just that I needed bail money that I would repay with interest within thirty minutes of my release.

The line stayed quiet for so long that I wondered if Jonas had hung up on me. I didn't want to call his name aloud, so I cleared my throat to prompt him. He requested another minute to devise a plan. At last, he told me he would send an "associate" with bail money. His connection would follow me to my apartment to pick up his reimbursement. When the deal culminated, I was to delete his number from my phone. Jonas's businesslike tone heaped on the guilt. Twice, he had helped me escape Stearns and the repercussions of continuing the association. I wish I dared to tell him of my plan to leave Richardson the next day, but he wouldn't have believed it. I was in a quandary.

THE FOLLOWING DAY, I marched myself into the army recruiter's office. My plan was to lie low until my court date a month later and ship out to basic training at the earliest possible minute afterward. Even though my apartment was close to Larry and Bertice's house, I had never mentioned it to them. I parked my truck in a spot they couldn't see from the road, but it occurred to me he may have noticed my truck already and tracked me to the bar from my apartment. I moved it anyway when I returned from the recruiter's office, hoping he hadn't tracked down my specific apartment.

It never occurred to me that the army would reject me. I always thought they took every able-bodied person willing to sign on the dotted line. Rejections were for poor eyesight and bad hearing and such. I understood they reveled at the idea of taking street fighters and making disciplined soldiers out of them. I wasn't a fighter—more of a street rat—but I could provide the military with a challenge. It turns out experienced recruiters can see right through the ruse of a good-for-nothing thirty-something desiring nothing the U.S. Army offered but the bus ride out of town. I was taken aback when the sergeant called with the army's rejection. The wave of disappointment soon passed, replaced by fear.

I figured Stearns would piece together another drug network as soon as he had any money. The same lack of cash that made him so angry with me was also the reason he wouldn't be scheduling a hit in my near future. I had to figure out a way to deliver him some quick cash to save my hide before he came after me. After that, I needed a strategy to pay him back the money I had taken. My only way out of this pickle was for Stearns to go back to prison for violating his parole and somehow avoid jail time myself. With over half of the little money I had remaining, I hired an attorney to make sure of the latter.

After avoiding Stearns for a month, I showed up at court dressed in the best suit and shoes the second-hand store in Garland near my lawyer's office offered. The guy staring at me from the mirror resembled... well, not me. His hair was short and neat, and he was so clean shaven that his face burned after a heavy dose of after shave. An outsider might have mistaken him for a corporate America middle manager. He had followed his lawyer's instructions to a tee, even though it took another chunk of his dwindling savings. To the judge, however, I might as well have dressed in clear plastic. He saw right through me.

MY CLEAN-CUT VICTIM routine may have worked on another judge but not on Judge Melvin Martinez. He was the judge I had promised would never see me in his courtroom again after he cut me loose from drug charges before sending the Stearnses to prison. When the bailiff read the names of the litigants in our disturbing the peace case, Judge Martinez glared over his half glasses at me and then at Stearns and back at me.

"Mr. Gull, if I remember correctly, you assured me if I let you off that other charge, you would get your own place, and I wouldn't see you in my courtroom again."

"Yes, your honor," I responded, standing. "And you

wouldn't have if Mr. Stearns hadn't burst into the bar where I was shooting pool, not bothering a soul, and punched me in the face." Judge Martinez asked me if I was drunk on the night in question, and I told him I was drinking my first beer of the night. He pressed for the reason for our fight. I wish he had asked Stearns, who would take great care to minimize the source of the conflict. Not wanting to reveal any more than was already in the police report, I told the judge that Stearns said I owed him money.

The police report from the first incident listed the amount of drugs seized in the raid, but it also made note that the police seized about two thousand dollars. The judge read that part of the report and remarked, "Seems like with that big of an operation, there might have been a lot more money sitting around the house somewhere. Is that the money to which we're referring, gentlemen?" I didn't respond, and neither did Stearns. I ached to steal a glance at Stearns while the judge was staring him down, but I figured the judge was baiting us to confirm his suspicions, so my eyes focused straight ahead.

Judge Martinez shifted his attention back to me and asked me where I was living. I gave him my address, though announcing it with Stearns in the room gave me pause. He asked how often I frequented Jernigan's, so I told him several times a week. He asked again if I was drunk on the night of my fracas with Stearns. I assured him I wasn't, that I only drank two or three beers when I went there and that I walked from my apartment. His questions pointed toward my drinking, but he was attempting to get me talking by asking questions he didn't think I would mind answering. By the time he switched directions in his interrogation, it was too late.

Judge Martinez's next question concerned whether I held current employment. I informed him I was between jobs, which was true. I just didn't tell him how long it had been since my last gainful employment. He pressed and asked what I did in my last job. I said I worked on the dock at a trucking company. He kept coming, asking if I had worked a job since moving to Texas. I admitted I hadn't had anything full-time. He asked about the amount of my rent. I told him six hundred dollars a month. He asked if I made a regular habit of eating, to which I laughed and answered in the affirmative. He wanted to know if I was receiving government assistance. At that point I sensed where he was going with his questioning, and I almost lied, but he could have uncovered that information without much difficulty. He figured my expenses—rent, utilities, food, and a few beers several times a week at the neighborhood bar—cost me about $1,500 a month. He asked if that sounded correct, and I told him "more or less."

The judge did some scribbling on some paper he had in front of him, and then he looked back up at me over his glasses. "So, Mr. Gull, by my math, it has cost you at least $90,000 to live these past five years. More or less. On the income side of the ledger, you have done some part-time work that you can't quite put your finger on since your arrival in Texas. Son, those numbers don't add up." I told him I hustled pool sometimes and that I had sold my boat and truck—partially true. Of course, I had sold the boat before I ever left Harriston to move out here. And the truck—I hadn't sold it yet, but it was the only item of value I had left.

My answer didn't satisfy him. He snickered and retorted, "Must have been a yacht for you to live for five years on the proceeds. Either that or you're mighty good at pool. How did you acquire this particular boat?" The question caught me off guard.

I stammered, "My ex-wife bought it for me."

The judge said he found that hard to believe, just like he found it hard to believe that a boat and a truck fetched more or less $90,000. He finally included Stearns in the conversation again. "So, I'll ask you again, gentlemen: What money were you fighting about?" When neither of us answered, he fined us $500 apiece for fighting in public and proposed I pay both fines, all but accusing me of stealing from Stearns.

My head was spinning when my attorney and I walked out of the courtroom. He should have been ashamed of himself for taking my money and not lifting an objection to help me when the judge started in on me. He suggested that if what the judge insinuated was true, I should pay the fines and give Stearns everything I could muster. Even when I told him he wouldn't get paid the rest of his fee for a while if I chose that route, he pushed me to do it. He wanted nothing to do with a drug operation. Neither did I, but I figured I was looking at a reckoning in the days to come. I told my lawyer I would pay for myself and for Stearns, and he arranged it with the court. He never sent a bill for the rest of my legal fees.

4

With no money left and nowhere to run, I agreed to meet with Larry Stearns and come to an understanding that wouldn't land either of us before Judge Melvin Martinez again. Stearns was more amenable when I slid him an envelope containing $5,000 across the table at a burger joint where we agreed to meet. My truck sold earlier that day for a few months' rent and some grocery money.

"That's a start," Stearns grumbled.

"You'll get the rest, I promise," I lied. I had no intention of paying him if I could devise an escape plan. I should have driven as far as the last tank of gas in my truck would take me and lived in my truck, far from the life I finally regretted. If you've read this far, though, you know my life wasn't exactly littered with wise choices. My life came to an impasse with no vehicle or place to drive if I owned one. Larry Stearns offered me a key to a future without him looking over my shoulder.

"What would happen if you couldn't pay your bill here in this restaurant?"

"I guess I'd call a friend and ask him to bring some money."

"Who would you call?" I couldn't tell whether he was fishing for accomplices or simply pointing out how friendless I was.

"Nobody."

"That's right, because who wants to help a lowlife who would steal a hardworking man's money? So how would you pay your bill?"

"I guess I'd see if they'd let me wash dishes—work it off."

"That's exactly what you're going to do for me, Brandon, work it off. And I have a prime location picked out for you—high risk, high reward. You'll work off your debt to me as fast as you can imagine. Or you'll go to jail. Or some punk will kill you. Makes no difference to me."

Two days later, I walked around the track behind the high school down the street, building a new clientele. My misery reached an all-time high a month later when I ran the numbers. Fifty thousand dollars divided by my take minus rent minus food minus Stearns's take, and paying him off would take years. I had no vehicle, no hope, and no marketable skills, save for some illicit sales ability. For one of the few times since choosing to steal drug money, I thought of Paula and the different life I could have lived with her. That was absurd, though. I chose my path to rock bottom by quitting her and walking away from my children, who I now hoped would never know me.

Once again, I settled into the path of least resistance in order to keep Stearns off my back. This time, I did it by working double shifts to speed his repayment as much as possible. With its three thousand students, the high school a few blocks from my apartment made for a ready market. Almost as if the school system and community leaders had collaborated to proffer the drug trade, the track between the school and the athletic fields was open for the community use in the evenings. Many of the students huddled there in the morning and between classes, so I shaved and dressed in the latest styles in order to frequent the track undetected during school hours.

A steady stream of clients kept me busy during the mornings. In a public school that size, I discovered, the right hand rarely knows what the left hand is doing. Administrators and students remained lulled into a sense of safety because an old, semi-retired police officer ate doughnuts with the teachers and yucked it up with the students. Meanwhile, students took regular trips to the bathroom with a detour around the walking track with their favorite drug dealer. I made myself scarce during afternoon hours when the sports teams practiced. Coaches would be the most likely to notice someone lurking around the place every day and also the most likely to run me off, so I ventured home for a nap during practice time. During the early evening hours, I would return to the track to walk a mile or two with companions who tagged out every lap.

Had it not been for the money I owed Stearns, I could have made a killing selling drugs at the school. As it was, though, I kept enough for rent, food, clothes, and a few other necessities and gave the rest to him. The funny thing is, this lazy bum enjoyed the exercise and even miss it on rainy days. Within a few months, I was in the best physical shape of my life, energized for occasional activity beyond my sales territory. I recorded every payment to Stearns in a notebook and gave him an index card containing my remaining balance with his money each week.

Stearns didn't ride me hard during the next few years. Neither did he extend an invitation to continue to partner with him after I repaid my debt. He understood the difficulty of my continued presence on the high school campus without detection. I understood that if anyone caught me selling drugs on school property, the judge would show no mercy. If I appeared before Judge Martinez again on drug charges, he would throw me under the jail. The tension between my risk and Stearns's reward kept our relationship copacetic, though neither of us trusted the other.

While I worked myself into physical shape walking the track, I contemplated my transition into a lower-paying profession, though I didn't know what it would be. It shouldn't threaten prison every day, for starters. As my remaining balance to Stearns dipped, I became more serious about finding honorable work. The saddest part of my story to that point was that I knew one person of integrity in the Dallas metroplex whom I could call, but Jonas wasn't answering. I never imagined that my path toward honest work would begin with a church sign.

ONE SATURDAY, about three months before I would pay off my debt to Stearns in full, I left the walking track, drug pocket empty and cash pocket full. I crossed the street to walk the half-mile to my apartment. At the church across the street from the school's tennis courts, I stopped to watch a guy changing the letters on the church sign. The message was intriguing, so I waited on the sidewalk twenty yards away for him to finish.

Looking for a Way to Escape Your Rut?

Recovery Ministry Starts This Week

Every Friday Night at 6:00, Holidays Included

Come Hungry, Leave Full

The sign in front of the church shouted different messages to passersby each week, but none of the other missives resonated with me like this one. My routine had become more fixed and unfulfilling than ever, even with my regular exercise. I couldn't stand my self-inflicted isolation any longer.

When the middle-aged gentleman fitting the letters into place stepped back to proofread his work, he caught me staring at the sign. "Does that question apply to you, friend?"

I stammered, "Me, no, well, maybe." I wondered how many times this sign engineer had changed the sign through the years.

"I'm Kerry Hapstead. Most folks call me Happy."

That forced a smile. "Nobody has ever accused me of that."

"Didn't catch your name."

"Brandon. Brandon G—Brandon Wade." I couldn't tell you what prompted me to give him my middle name instead of my surname, but it felt clean, new.

"Nice to meet you, Brandon Wade. If you need a friendly face to make you feel welcome, you'll find me here every Friday night. God delivered me when everybody else had given up on me. I'm living proof that you're never too far gone."

"Delivered you from what?"

"Tell you what, come Friday night and hear for yourself. I'll be giving my testimony—sorry, that's church talk for telling my story—to kick off our new season of recovery ministry. I'd love for you to be my guest."

"Maybe I will."

"You know, Brandon, Friday is six days away still. How about I tell you part of my story today and hope it's enough to draw you back on Friday night? Buy you lunch?"

"No thanks. I was about to head back…"

"Come on, my treat. I'm not taking no for an answer. There's a Whataburger around the corner."

While covering the short distance to his heavy-duty pickup in the parking lot, I tried my best to make conversation. "That's one thing I love about Texas."

"What's that?"

"Whataburger."

"Don't have 'em where you're from, do they?"

"Nope."

"Where's home, Brandon?"

"I don't know that home is anywhere, really. But I came to Texas from Harriston, Mississippi."

"Can't say I've ever had the pleasure. What brought you to Texas?"

Before I could capture the words springing forth from my inmost being, they had escaped. "Quitting. Running. Story of my life, Happy, what there is of it."

"Like a rut that you can't get out of no matter how hard you try?"

"Exactly like that, only I couldn't even convince myself that I've tried very hard."

Happy pulled up to the stop sign around the corner from the restaurant. "Brandon, ten years ago I said words so similar to what you just said that it's eery. I'll be honest with you—it doesn't matter how hard you try. Unless you let go of control of your life and let God have it, you stand little chance of becoming who you want to be. Take it or leave it, that's how I see it."

I sat without speaking, wanting to move toward this guy with the magnetic nickname and at the same time considering throwing open the passenger door and bolting away from him. His next words called me back.

"I'm not looking to judge you or anybody else, so please don't think that. It's just—well, God delivered me from my sin and myself. I dedicated my life to letting Him use me to draw others like me away from their self-centered lives toward the lives He wants for them. For all of us. Free from guilt and shame."

We sat in the Whataburger parking lot, neither of us reaching for our door handle. My conflicting emotions were tearing at me from every angle. He was giving them time to sort themselves out before we entered the restaurant. I found the confidence to take the next step, a confidence fueled by smells wafting across the asphalt.

"YOU A PREACHER?" I asked, sliding my tray onto the table.

"Not per se. I own an electrical company. That's a story in itself."

"I'm not busy the rest of today. Let's hear it."

Kerry Hapstead took a bite from his burger, washed it down with a sip of root beer, and traveled back to his day of reckoning. Starting with a motorcycle wreck on his way home from his job as an electrician's apprentice, he allowed pain medication to give way to opioids. His downturn was steady, costing him his job eight months after the wreck. On the verge of renting his first apartment, he moved instead into his parents' basement. Two unsuccessful rehab stints at their expense later, they revoked his welcome. He understood that his eighty-year-old grandmother was his last stop before homelessness, levity that kept him clean for two weeks before the drugs came calling again. His father monitored his every move in his mother's house, pressing charges and booting him to the street when Happy pilfered from his grandma's cookie jar.

With no job and no home, Happy turned to burglary to fund his drug habit. He found copper tubing on church air conditioning units an easy target, but when the police caught him, they connected him to other burglaries he had committed. After and year-and-a-half in jail, he walked out with the clothes on his back, a bus ticket back to Dallas, and his hard-won sobriety. Happy didn't waste his time behind bars. A prison chaplain led him to the Lord and walked with him toward freedom from his addiction.

The same grandmother who had given Happy his last opportunity to turn his life around before he went to prison extended him a second chance. He responded by staying straight, working hard, and attending recovery meetings. A friend who had been a fellow intern before Happy's spiral had used the intervening years to earn his electrician's license. He took a chance by hiring his old friend, while Happy went to work on obtaining his own license through on-the-job training and night classes. Had he wanted to return to using drugs, he would have had to climb over fifty hours of work every week and nightly classes or recovery meetings. After church on Sundays, he napped.

Two years of this breakneck schedule later, Happy started a recovery ministry at the small church where I met him. In the last few years, he had started his own company and taken risks on a dozen young men trying to put their demons behind them. Before he dropped me off at my apartment, Happy doubled down on his invitation to come hear his story again and handed me a card with his business and personal contact information. I spent the rest of the weekend researching the path to a career as an electrician.

The day before I intended to take Happy up on his invitation, I was arrested on trespassing charges.

5

With weeks to go before I retired for good from the drug business, I made my first mistake since going back to work for Stearns. One of my regulars forgot his wallet for our usual Tuesday business meeting after lunch. He asked me to meet him back by the tennis courts after school, and I agreed. I shouldn't have, but he was a solid customer that I wanted to keep happy for another few months. The problem was, Tuesdays in the spring were busy sports days. I showed up early to meet my client, but several of my regulars were milling around and came over to chat and talk shop. A teacher sitting at a table taking up money near the softball field spotted me.

This teacher suspected I was dealing drugs on campus and called one of her principals. I glanced in her direction two or three times and sensed she was tracking my every move. I told the kids hanging around me to get lost, that we were being watched. When the principal arrived, I was still standing near the tennis courts waiting for my guy alone. He asked my purpose in loitering around his campus like a big shot. He told me to get lost, but I told him I was waiting for some friends to join me for the baseball game, which he didn't believe. After I didn't give him the response he wanted, he marched up the hill to talk to the teacher. I moved behind a tree where I could see them, but they couldn't see me. She gestured toward the spot I had been standing, mimicking my movements. The principal pulled out his cell phone and made a call, keeping an eye out for me.

I should have walked away and taken care about showing up again when outdoor sports were taking place with so many school officials on the grounds. I gave my customer five more minutes and then bolted for the track. The bathrooms for the baseball field were situated behind the stands on the opposite end of the track. To reach them, you walk around a wall that blocks the line of sight for anyone standing where the principal and teacher were still stalking me. On the other side of the baseball field is a row of thick hedges, a perfect place to hide my product where no one would find it.

Free from any incriminating evidence, I slipped back onto the track and walked laps with the thirty others exercising there. My regular joined me on my second lap, but I sent him away with instructions to meet me back there after dark. Sure enough, by the end of that lap, a police car pulled into the parking lot and after conferring with the principal, a uniformed officer made a beeline for me. He started with a demand to leave school property, but I stood my ground and asked why. Dozens of people were walking on the track like I was, and they weren't being escorted from the grounds. I shouldn't have been so stubborn, but we both knew he was too late to nab me doing anything illegal. After a few minutes of arguing back and forth, he gave me the choice of walking off campus on my accord or riding away in handcuffs. I couldn't help mouthing off one more time, so he cuffed me and arrested me for trespassing.

I used my phone call to ask Stearns to pick me up from the police station, which he did not. When my court date arrived, I was sweating bullets, hoping not to spend time in the company of one Judge Melvin Martinez. To my great relief, I appeared before another judge, where I made the case that the police officer arrested me for doing what "forty or fifty" other people were doing at the same time as I was. I chatted with "a few friends of my nephew's" and waited in vain for "my cousins to join me for my nephew's game." The judge never asked my nephew's name or if I was conducting any other business on the school campus. He just threw out the case, more eager to clear his docket than to delve into my comings and goings.

Stearns couldn't have cared less about my court appointment. He didn't expect me to last as long as I did without going to prison, but I had paid him back in full and was working on the interest he considered his due. The cops were on to me, though, and I had neither the nerve nor the motivation to walk on those grounds again. I would not risk moving to another location for a few weeks. I told Stearns I quit, that he could sue me for his so-called interest if he wanted. He laughed at me and told me he didn't think I had it in me to stick around as long as I did. Then, he suggested no one would find my body if I ratted him out now or ever. It was tough guy talk he didn't have the guts to enforce, and we both knew it by that point in our relationship. Still, I walked away from the drug trade, alive and clear from obligation. Unusual, I understand, but that's how it happened. I walked straight to the barbershop, paid for a clean haircut and shave, and embarked on my new life.

MY FIRST CALL was to Kerry Hapstead.

"Hello?"

"Hey, uh, Happy, this is..."

"Brandon, right?"

"Yeah. Wow, you remembered."

"Hey, good to hear from you, buddy. You doing okay?"

"Y-yeah, I suppose. Listen, I'm sorry I missed your—sorry, I forget what you called it."

"Testimony."

"Yeah, that. I wanted to come listen to you speak, but an emergency came up that afternoon."

"That's okay. Everything went off fine. It was a good night."

"But I still want to hear the rest of your story, if that's okay with you, that is."

"Of course, Brandon, of course. Hey, look, I don't mean to pry, but are you in some kind of trouble?"

"N-no, not really. Maybe I was the last time I talked to you, but I'm ready to make a new start. I just might need someone to point me in the right direction."

"Tell you what, Brandon. Why don't you meet me for church on Sunday morning, and we'll grab a bite to eat afterward. I can give you the afternoon to tell me how I can help. That sound good?"

"S-sure."

"You remember the church where we met, right across from the school. Meet me in the parking lot at 10:30 on Sunday morning. I'll walk out by my truck so I'll be easy for you to find."

"Yeah, sure, I'll see you then. And thanks, Happy."

"Yes, sir, glad to help. See you Sunday."

WHENEVER I SAW the light at the end of the tunnel in Texas, unexpected circumstances inevitably sideswiped me in those days. However, on this occasion, I met Happy at our prescribed time and walked into a church for the first time. The experience was not what I expected. I still had my second-hand suit from my court appearance for defending myself against Stearns. Worried about appearing slovenly, I overdressed, one of only three people in the place wearing a suit. One of those was the preacher, and even he wore an open collar. Happy suggested I lose the tie and toss it back in my vehicle, but I told him I'd keep it on this time. I couldn't muster the courage to tell him why I no longer owned a truck. At least not until later.

Happy was an intuitive sort who suggested we sit near the back so I could familiarize myself with the atmosphere of their church. When I assumed aloud that Happy had a family, he said they had attended the 9:00 service and left him to connect with me. I remember thinking Happy was the only soul in Richardson, Texas, who would make that effort for me. I wondered what else might be at work because that kind of luck just didn't follow me.

All the standing up and sitting down during the service kept me alert. About the time I would get settled into a comfortable position on one of the padded benches that looked an awful lot like courtroom benches, it was time to stand again. The singing was lively, but I didn't recognize any of the songs. I liked their hopeful tone, though, and made a mental note to ask Happy if the songs were available outside of church. The preacher announced he was going to pray, and the people bowed their heads like robots. Not understanding the custom, I didn't right away, and the preacher caught my eye. He smiled and nodded and then went about praying for the needs of people I assumed were church members. He prayed that some spirit would use his words and help us understand what God wanted to say to us. That was the Holy Spirit, I would later learn, but I admit his trust in a spirit I didn't understand freaked me out more than a little that first Sunday.

After the preacher closed the prayer, the people did

some kind of chant together. Happy leaned over and whispered that they said the Apostle's Creed every week to express what they believed about God. The need to recite it so often struck me as odd, but the people were so earnest that they inspired me to be firm in what I believed—whatever that turned out to be. After the recitation ended, they passed some baskets around and people put money in it. Some people put checks and others put fives, tens, twenties. Happy didn't put any money in the basket before he passed it to me and motioned me to pass it to the man who was taking the basket from row to row. I asked Happy later about the purpose of the money and why he didn't put any money in the basket. By then, he had figured out that many parts of my morning experience were an enigma. He assured me he had put a check in the basket during first service.

The longest we stayed in one place was when the preacher started talking. He read from the Bible, which Happy showed me how to download on my phone. I didn't figure phones were a part of church, but I was excited to have a copy of the Bible for free. The preacher talked about three stories from a book called Luke, which sounded like a rather short title for a book in the Bible. I discovered later that the Bible is comprised of quite a few books of different lengths, written over thousands of years. Luke was named as it was because a guy named Luke wrote it. I wondered why they didn't include his last name, but it seemed like a question I might embarrass myself to ask, so I asked Siri later. She didn't know, either, but I found the answer on my own.

In the process I discovered that Jesus's last name wasn't *Christ*, but that it was some kind of title.

That Sunday in church revealed an entire world about which I had no idea. I realized a preacher can talk to an entire room and one person at the same time. He told stories from that Luke book about people finding lost things—a sheep, a coin, and a son. I admit I was a little confused by the first two stories, but the third one hit me square between the eyes. I was the lost son, and God was the father who inexplicably wanted to welcome me home, whatever *home* was. The preacher somehow recognized it, too, because he kept making eye contact with me. When he summed up his sermon, he pointed out that the lost sheep and lost coin didn't decide to be found, but that people can realize their lostness and decide to be found. I found myself longing to be found—whatever that meant.

At the end of his talk, the preacher asked everybody to bow their heads and close their eyes. I leaned forward this time, but not before catching him glancing in my direction again. He poured his heart into asking lost people to come forward to talk to some people standing up front about "being saved." I only had a slight notion what he was talking about, but several people stood up and walked to the front. My heart seemed ready to pound out of my chest, though, which distracted me from what the preacher was saying. What a fine first impression, I considered, to pass out from a heart attack while the church focused on God in that moment. I told Happy that afternoon about my heart beating so fast, and he laughed and informed me I had been "under conviction." I wondered how God knew about my conviction and what else he understood about me. The experience was confusing but wonderful. My afternoon with Happy might not allow enough time for all my questions.

6

"Did you grow up going to church?" Happy asked after we had ordered our lunch at a sit-down restaurant, the likes of which I had not frequented since I was with Paula.

"Where I grew up, there was a Baptist church on every corner." Something inside me held back the entire truth that my first personal experience inside a church had happened moments before. Happy was familiar with addicts' habit of skirting the truth. While not a drug addict, my behavior was similar. He let the silence beg the whole truth. "My family didn't go to church when I was a kid, so I didn't go when I moved out on my own."

"Didn't go, as in..."

"At all."

"Brandon, was this your first time to attend a church?"

Bull's eye. I shifted my eyes to meet his and nodded, ashamed.

"Weddings, funerals?"

"No. I went to the justice of the peace to get married, and I'm not exactly close to my family. Kind of the black sheep, you might say."

"Brandon, have you ever been skydiving?"

I perceived the abrupt change of direction had some purpose, so I followed along. "No."

"But there's no shame in not skydiving for you. Your response was matter-of-fact. When I asked you about church, you dodged the question at first and then guilt pressed in on you when I pushed the issue. Why do you think that is?"

I said I wasn't sure, though I was confident Happy was. He seemed to stay a step ahead of my thoughts.

"It's because you don't have an innate inner longing to sky dive. Sure, some people like the adrenaline rush of jumping out of a perfectly operational plane, but it's not universal. However, with God, everyone longs to relate to Him somehow. According to God's Word in the Bible, He created humans in His image. Adam and Eve were the original people, and for a short time, they walked and talked with God. Temptation came, though, and they disobeyed the one limitation God had placed on them. Theologically—that is, the study of God—God called their choice to go their own way *sin*, and all of humanity has been struggling with it ever since."

My plate of roast beef and vegetables that seemed so appetizing earlier now served as an outlet for my nervous energy. I rearranged the peas and corn and moved them back again as Happy spoke. As he gauged my response, I mumbled how I was familiar enough with temptation. He smiled and promised me I was not alone, that he struggled with various forms of it every day. That someone could be as confident and content as Happy without completely overcoming temptation gave me hope.

"My road to where I am now was not a simple route, but I haven't gotten to the gospel yet."

"Gospel?"

"That's a word in the Bible which literally means 'good news.' Church people sometimes use it to talk about anything related to God, but it means the birth, life, ministry, death, and resurrection of Jesus, God's Son. After Adam and Eve disobeyed God and sin entered the world, humankind rebelled more and more against God. There was this big gulf we couldn't cross to get back to God, even though He gave His people many rules to follow to please him, starting with the ten commandments. The rules showed man how to follow God, but what they did at the same time was to show our inability to please God in our own strength. And since the Bible also teaches that the price of our sin is both physical death and spiritual death, being separated from our Creator forever is the end result of sin. Brandon, is there anyone from whom you are estranged, and you're positive it's your fault?"

I snickered and informed him the list was long.

"Give me one name."

"Paula, my ex-wife. I guess, technically, she's still… anyway, her name is Paula."

"Okay, fine, we'll use Paula."

I snickered again. "I've done plenty of that."

Happy stopped to smile at his word choice, but he was going somewhere with his line of questioning, so I urged him to continue.

"What if it wasn't possible—zero chance—to apologize and make amends with Paula? How would you feel?"

"It is that way, and I carry the weight of being a rotten human being. She was young and rebellious when we met, but she grew into a responsible, mature adult after our daughter was born. Suffice it to say I didn't."

"What if all hope—every shred—was gone for forgiveness and redemption?"

"After what I've done to her…" He cut me off.

"Let's not get lost in the weeds, Brandon. What if you could stand in front of Paula and say, 'I'm sorry?' What if you could say, 'I was wrong, I don't deserve it, but would you forgive me?'"

"Oh, I could never do that."

"Why not?"

"Too ashamed, I guess."

"And there you have it." Happy sat back, satisfied he had delivered me to… wherever I was.

"What do you mean?"

"God created man, man sinned against God, and man's shame makes him reluctant to humble himself before God. But do you know who has the ultimate power to forgive man from his sin and restore man to Himself?"

"God?"

"Yes, God. Now, here's God's dilemma, though God has never had to figure out a problem. God is perfect, holy, set apart. Sin cannot enter His presence, and humans are sinful. As a righteous judge, God must sentence us to the consequence assigned to sin, and that's death. Brandon, I'm assuming from some things you've said that you've spent time in a courtroom?"

I nodded.

"Are you familiar with the term *loophole* in the law?"

"Yeah, a technicality that gets you off for a punishment you deserve."

"Perfect. God left a loophole in His law, so to speak. Only, loopholes in our law arise from poorly written laws or some technicality the lawmakers didn't consider. God's loophole was His plan from before the foundation of the world. God knew people would sin, leaving them unable to return to Him, their Creator. He understands that quivering in your gut right now, Brandon, because He put it there to draw you back to Him. He's aware of how incapable we are of paying the debt we owe Him. Tell me, what's the biggest debt you've ever owed?"

"Seventy grand that I stole from a drug dealer." The words escaped before I could filter them and they set Happy back a stride.

"Hmm, I'd be interested in hearing that story later. Did you pay it back?"

"Every dime."

"I bet it seemed like you'd never get it paid off, right?"

"You can only imagine."

"What if yours was a perpetual debt made greater by passing time?"

"*I* can only imagine."

"You already have a greater understanding of debt than most people with whom I share this. You understand the bondage of owing somebody more than you believe you can pay."

"Do I ever."

"But you have also experienced the freedom from that bondage. How did you feel after you made your last payment?"

"You said it, a kind of free that was like the weight of the world being lifted from my shoulders. Too many times, I was close to falling so deep in a hole that I couldn't find my way out. The day I met you was one of those days. When I think about how close I was to jail at any moment over the past ten years, I shake. I didn't have any hopes and dreams, really, but I sure didn't want to spend any part of my life in a prison cell."

"So when the pastor was talking about being lost today, did you understand what it meant for us to be lost spiritually?"

"Kind of, because this sort of grip on my innards wouldn't let go. Does that make sense?"

"Oh, yeah. That's God bringing conviction to your heart. Happened to me, too."

Happy laughed when I asked how God knew about my conviction, but he set me straight. "I bet that even though you stole money from a drug dealer, you still sense a certain guilt about it. Am I right?"

"Yeah, I understood the consequences. And I guess I understood it was wrong."

"If you felt guilty about doing wrong to a drug dealer, how much more when you offend a holy God who is without sin?"

"I don't figure I'd have much of a shot of paying him back what I owe."

"You're right, but He understands that, too. That's why He sent His Son to die on a cross to take our place. See, when God established His law, He communicated to man that the price for sin was death. Only the death of a sinless person would satisfy His price for sin, and no one on earth qualified. Jesus lived a perfect life, though, so He qualified. He didn't deserve to die, but He stepped in to take our place like an innocent man stepping in to take a prison sentence for someone who deserved to die in jail."

I grew quiet, contemplating what Happy was telling me and trying to synthesize it with the turbulence churning in my gut.

"Brandon," he said, his voice scarcely above a whisper. "You need Jesus to save you from your sins. He has already accepted your sentence and paid the price. He's calling you to accept His payment. His offer runs out when you die. Somebody will pay for your sins, either you or Him. Who's it going to be?"

I choked out, "Him. What do I have to do?"

"Follow Him. It's more than just praying a prayer. It's trusting His payment but then following Him, helping lead others to Him."

"Like you're doing right now."

"Exactly like that."

"And you'll help me?"

Happy nodded, let me pray some awkward words of my own, and celebrated when I finished. And then he offered me a job.

7

Happy's offer wasn't a handout, though he told me we would spend a week working through the paperwork before I took my drug test, even after I assured him I could pass right away. Given his history of helping addicts, I couldn't fault the guy for being careful. A week later, on a Monday morning bright and early, I began my career as a general flunkie for Happy Electric after hitching a ride to work with the boss. Happy introduced me to a guy named Jacob, who led a crew of now three. Jacob was clean cut but armed with tattoos up and down both arms. He smiled at me like he knew something I didn't and gripped my hand with both of his.

"Glad to have you on board, Brandon." After the owner walked toward his office, Jacob gestured toward Happy and said, "So, you and Happy…"

"I'm not an addict," I answered without emotion.

He backed up half a step and threw up his hands.

"Not judging, man. Of all the crews driving smily faced trucks all over Dallas today, you'll find the least judgment on this one. I would be dead if it hadn't been for Kerry Hapstead. That man saved my life. Well, Jesus saved my life, but He used Happy to do it. Brandon, do you… have you…?"

"Last Sunday."

"All right, all right then, brother, welcome aboard!" Jacob grabbed my hand and shook it again. "Hey, this is my partner, C.J. I'm sure he'll tell you his story at some point today, but we'd better get going. I hope you're a hard worker, Brandon, because you can do well for yourself in this company if you don't mind the work."

"I'll be honest with you, Jacob, I've spent my adult life running from hard work and responsibility. Back in the day, I had a decent job on the dock of a trucking company, but it was pretty tough work some days. I squirreled away that opportunity, though. That was a long time ago. This is my second, third, fourth chance at making something of myself, and I'm determined not to blow it this time."

"Look, if you feel lightheaded out there today, you let us know. Happy didn't assign you to us to break you in the hard way or anything like that. We grind it every day and come back to the shop satisfied that we've done our boss proud. And Happy, too, if you know what I mean."

"But I thought he was the boss."

"Happy's the boss here, but he's not Lord. C.J. and me—we've agreed that we're going to do what the Bible says and do everything as unto the Lord. We've had a solid run of satisfied customers, so we hope you'll help us keep up our streak. Another thing—during our lunch hour, we grab a bite to eat and do a little Bible study. You down with that?"

"Sure. Happy gave me a Bible, but I didn't bring it with me."

"You got a phone?"

"Yeah."

"Let me see it."

I unlocked it and handed it to him. He punched a few buttons and handed my phone back. "So you already have the app. Not as convenient as a paper Bible for writing notes, but you always have the Word with you. Now, let's get going. C.J., do we have everything we need for the Clevinger job?"

"Loaded and ready."

"All right, load up." As we pulled off the lot, Jacob previewed the job. "We're installing light fixtures in a building under construction this morning. We've already run the wires—you'll learn how to do that another time."

"Do you ever—" I started, "I mean, is it dangerous?"

"Working with electricity, you mean?"

"Yeah, it can kill you, right?"

"If you don't know what you're doing, sure. Don't worry, though, we'll take care of you."

C.J. laughed and added, "Not a lot of danger carrying boxes and cleaning up like you'll be doing while you see if this is what you want to do. I started where you are a year ago. It's not too bad, just boiling hot on some days. Make sure you pre-hydrate because once you start sweating, you can't catch up, no matter how much you drink. I learned that the hard way."

"How do you mean?"

"I spent ten years of my life holding a bottle, but drinking enough water was new to me. I guess it had been, what, three or four days, Jacob?" His partner nodded. "So we had spent the first days I was here replacing ceiling fans, changing out some interior light fixtures, stuff like that. All inside work in air-conditioned houses. Then, we wired a house under construction, and I drank coffee for the better part of the morning. We got busy, and I started feeling lightheaded. I figured it was because I hadn't done much physical activity for so long, but the lightheadedness gave way to dizziness. Jacob sent me out to the truck for some wire. When I didn't come back in the next few minutes, he climbed down from his ladder and came to check on me. The next thing I remember was waking up with an EMT standing over me. I spent the next few hours in a hospital with an IV stuck in my arm. It was embarrassing to leave the job in an ambulance, let me tell you."

"He returned work the next morning," Jacob intervened. "That's when Happy knew he was a keeper. He's been doing solid work ever since."

"I'm what you call an apprentice," C.J., rising to his full height. "That means I work with Jacob during the day and attend classes at night to learn the business."

"He can do pretty much everything I can do now."

"Yeah, because the on-the-job training prepares you more than the schooling does."

I took it all in, expecting to follow in C.J.'s footsteps after researching the electrical field and the path to making it a viable career. Happy was the first man I could point to as a role model, and I wanted to make him proud of me.

I SURVIVED the first week of working with Jacob and C.J. They seemed surprised every new day I showed up for work and kept up with them all day long. Until one day they didn't. I can't pinpoint the day or even say that anything specific clicked in them, but we soon fell into a groove. Happy still drove me to work most days. Over several months, I told him my life story, the little good and the lot of bad. He didn't speak most mornings, just listened and nodded. It seemed he took a particular liking to Paula as I shared our struggles. Perhaps he sympathized with her because I didn't sugarcoat how wrong I was to treat her like I did. Every once in a while, after C.J. started picking me up for work, he would catch me at the shop and ask a question, often about Paula or our children. He'd nod and thank me for sharing and tuck away what I had told him in the recesses of his mind. He never forgot a thing.

At lunch every day, Jacob walked C.J. and me through one book of the Bible after another. I discovered C.J. had not grown up going to church, either. He seemed to understand the Bible better than I did, but everything he had learned had come in the previous year of working and doing Bible study with Jacob.

Every night, Jacob assigned us to read a chapter or two from a book of the Bible. We started with John, which was weird because I had never started two-thirds of the way through a book. Jacob said that it would give me the best picture of who Jesus was and that we could build out from there. So we started with John, and twenty-one days later, I had read through my first book of the Bible. I felt like I had accomplished something until I flipped through the Bible Happy had given me and found that Psalms had 150 chapters.

Jacob encouraged C.J. and me during lunch every day that the key to understand Scripture was to keep showing up. Showing up each night to read a new chapter and ask for God's help in understanding it. Showing up at our daily Bible studies to talk about what we had learned with other believers. Showing up to church on Sundays to hear a pastor who had studied a text all week talk about it. Learning God's Word seemed daunting at first, but I kept doing what Jacob said. As one day turned into another and one question turned into another, I was less and less shaky on the wobbly legs of my newfound faith. Happy checked in on me occasionally during the week and often on weekends. He seemed satisfied with my progress.

"BRANDON, I need you to step into my office for a few minutes." Happy sounded so businesslike that my reflexes told me I was in some kind of trouble. Though I hadn't made a mistake on the job in a while, maybe he was going to call me down for forgetting a drill on the roof of the Clayborne job a month earlier. I had breathed a sigh of relief when we returned a day later and found it in the same spot where I left it. Nevertheless, it had been careless of me to leave it. I would have paid for the drill if it had been missing or hadn't worked. Jacob told me it was no big deal, so I forgot about it until Happy told me to close the door to his office.

"Brandon, do you know what today is?"

"Uh, Friday?"

"Right, this week, but what I mean is that you've been with Happy Electric for a year today."

"Man," I said, relaxing, "that was sudden. It seems like just a few months ago you introduced me to Jacob and C.J."

"You like it here?"

"Oh, yeah, I love it. I can't thank you enough for giving me this job and putting me with the crew you did. I don't have anything to compare it to, but I think Jacob and C.J. and me work well together."

"You do, you do." Happy had something else on his mind, and he seemed reluctant to share it with me.

"Is everything okay, boss?"

"Brandon, C.J. is leaving us to take a job with another company. His wife's company transferred her to Tulsa, Oklahoma, and C.J. wasn't real excited about a four-hour commute every day. We helped him land a spot with an outfit up there that's going to be pleased to employ someone of C.J.'s caliber, both as a worker and as a person. You didn't meet him until he was a full year into recovery, but I'm sure you're well aware of his story by now. He's a new man."

"For sure."

"Anyway, I understand you depend on him for rides back and forth to work."

"Yeah, but I'll work out something. I'm planning on getting something of my own soon. I just haven't been able to save enough yet."

"So, I'm not paying you enough to buy your own ride—is that what you're telling me?"

His rebuke stung. "No, I wasn't saying…"

Happy cut me off with a wave of his hand and a grin. "Not where I was going. How about we take care of both of your issues in one fell swoop?"

"Huh?"

"How do you like the new work truck I assigned y'all last week?"

"Nice, rides good. The old truck was fine, though. It never let us down."

"That's good to hear because I want you to drive the old truck for your new position."

"Huh?"

"Brandon, you've done outstanding work over this past year. The guys around the shop like you, and Jacob and C.J. brag on your work ethic. I don't pay my new guys much more than enough to survive for the first year to give them time to prove themselves. More than that, though, they need to show me they're putting their old lives behind them. After a year of begging rides, I have full confidence the drug business won't entice you back."

I stretched to my full height in my chair. "No way, no how, no, sir."

He smiled and nodded. "Good. I want you to take the truck, clean it up real good, and drive it wherever you need to go. Make sure you remember that wherever you go in it, that happy-faced logo goes with you, as does the reputation of our company."

"Thanks, I..."

Happy held up his hand. "There's more. I want you to step into a new position that I need filled. Our crews spend way too much of their day running back to the shop for something they forgot or something that they need for their jobs that they don't have on their trucks. I want you to be a runner for us. If one of our guys needs something from the shop, his crew keeps right on working while you deliver what they need. Sound like something you can do?"

"Sure, but..."

"Comes with a raise."

"Thanks, but..."

"What is it?"

"Nothing. I'm glad to do whatever you need me to do, Happy. I'll just miss lunch with Jacob and C.J. Did you know we've studied over twenty books of the Bible this past year?"

"I did. And I want you near Jacob's crew every day for the next year at lunchtime, still studying the Word together. I want you to start with John."

"We already did that one."

"I want you to start over with Roger. I met Roger two weeks ago at our recovery group at church, and I offered him a job this week. Jacob's my best disciple-maker, so I assigned Roger to his crew. I didn't realize C.J. would be moving, so Jacob will get a new apprentice. I don't want him to have to break in two right-hand men, so you're going to be his discipleship right arm, okay? Think you're ready to graduate into that position, too?"

"I'll give it a shot."

"I was sure I could count on you."

"Thanks, Happy. I'll do my best." I stood to leave.

"One more thing, Brandon. I don't know why the Lord won't leave me alone about this, but I want to ask you about something else."

8

"Brandon, do you trust me?"

"More than anybody else in my life." I didn't recognize what this turn in the conversation meant, but everything so far had been for my benefit.

"What I'm about to ask you borders on meddling, but we're far enough into our discipleship relationship that I'm going to say it. I also get that one of our weekend restaurant visits might be a better venue than work, but, trust me, this effects nothing I already offered you."

"You're killing me, Happy. Just ask already. I promise not to get mad at you."

Happy leaned back in his high-backed office chair and placed his hands behind his head. "You may have noticed I've asked you several times about Paula?"

"Oh, yeah." Happy had been inching ever close to the full truth about my ill-fated marriage, and I was nearing complete transparency with him.

"Brandon, I've been piecing parts of your story together for months, and there's part of it missing."

"My divorce."

"Yep."

"We never divorced. I told you I bailed and never looked back. It's not something I'm proud of, Happy, but I ran out on my wife and kids without leaving Paula so much as a forwarding address. As far as I know, she doesn't realize I'm in Texas. She hasn't come running after me. Probably didn't have the money to pursue a divorce. I moved to Richardson and got caught up with Stearns and then stayed off the grid as much as possible until I met you that day in front of the church. With all I had on my mind, I didn't care to pursue another woman. Geez, that would have complicated my train wreck life even more."

"Do you still love your wife?" Happy redirected.

"I'm gonna be honest with you—I'm not sure I ever loved Paula. I think about her, sure, and I hate myself for what I did to her, to my daughter, to my son. Paula and I were both so young, but she was the best part of us. She grew up. I didn't. She was the more responsible one of us the entire time."

"Have you considered seeing if there's a way you could straighten things out with Paula?"

"You mean apologize?"

"As a start."

"I can't tell you how many times I've rehearsed it in my head. No words adequately express remorse for running out on your wife and kids with not so much as a word for twenty-plus years now."

"How long are you going to wait?"

"In my mind, when I go back to Harriston to find her, she's moved away or found somebody else." I paused before adding, "Or she hates me so bad that she runs after me with a baseball bat as soon as I show my face."

"But you don't know."

"No, but if you were her, would it give you a thrill to see me sauntering up your front walkway?"

"No, probably not. Perhaps you shouldn't *saunter*, as you say." He managed a slight grin, but for only a moment. "What if she's tired of playing mother and father and could use some validation that nothing she did drove you away? Or what if she has spent her anger already and wants to let bygones be bygones? What if she's ready for her kids to meet their daddy—better late than never? What if...?"

I picked up a shop towel to wave in concession. "Okay, I hear you, Happy. That could happen, but it's not likely, you must admit."

"Fair enough, but for every negative outcome you could throw out there, I can match you with a positive. My point is that you don't even know how she responded to your leaving, much less anything she's done or said or thought since then. You just don't know."

"You're right. That's a big step, Happy, one I'm not sure I'm ready to take."

"You've come a long way, Brandon. It's not my intention to push you too hard on this, but I had a feeling you had never divorced your wife. If that's what she wants, don't you think you owe her that much so she can move on with her life?"

"That's something I never considered. Maybe she's in love with some guy who wants to marry her but can't."

"You should at least reach out at some point. I don't want to rush you, but I didn't care to keep sidestepping the issue, either."

"I had an idea you were getting close to figuring out my deepest secret—at least the one that I haven't flat out told you. It's been haunting me, honestly, and I'm glad you brought it up. I wish I knew the best place to start."

"Social media?"

"I don't do that stuff. Anybody who cares about what's going in my life works with us or goes to church with us. I'm going to see them at least once a week anyway, so what's the point?"

"It might help you discover what's going on in Paula's life."

"Give me some time, would you, Happy? Let me think it through and be wise in how I approach it."

"I won't say another word."

"No need for a complete freeze, but give me some time, okay?"

"Done. Thanks for not going off on me for asking you about your marriage."

"Shoot, after everything you've done for me, the least I can do is answer some uncomfortable questions that are looking out for my good, anyway."

"Glad you see it that way. Lunch Sunday out at my place?"

"Sounds good."

"Julie and I need to deliver some food plates right after church, so meet us out there about one o'clock. You can do that since you'll have your own ride." He tossed me the keys to my Happy Electric work truck. "Make this one last you a year and we'll see about getting you in a new one from the next fleet."

Catching the keys and staring at them, I pried myself from my seat in Happy's office. C.J. was moving. Jacob was taking on a new disciple. My work performance satisfied Happy enough to give me a company truck and a raise. Paula, Lisa, and David were the great unknown. My stomach muscles tightened as I unlocked the driver's side door to Happy Electric truck number seventy-two.

TWO MONTHS LATER, I was back in court, this time of my own choosing. It was impulsive, but I wanted a tangible reminder of my break from an old life. Most people in my generation would have expressed it through a tattoo, but I didn't want to risk running into any remnants of my former life. Who am I kidding? My hatred of needles nixed that option before it gained any traction. I changed my name instead.

One week between books of the Bible, Jacob used our lunchtime Bible study to consider Bible characters whose names God changed: *Abram* to *Abraham, Sarai* to *Sarah, Jacob* to *Israel, Simon* to *Peter*. I offered *Saul* to *Paul,* but he said the Bible evidence just wasn't there to prove that God changed his name, just that he was "also called" *Paul*. Because our study fascinated me so much, I considered a new name for myself.

I would never try to convince anyone that my name change was God led, but I embraced my middle name that my cousins used to kid me about as a child. Though *Wade* is not an unusual name, they made it seem so by chanting "Wade in the water, Wade in the water" when we would get together to play. I detested their teasing and took to hating my middle name, too, but the ever-changing me liked it just fine. The name change cost less than a good tattoo, and I walked out of court as *Brandon Wade*, a new name for my new life.

SIX MONTHS PASSED after Happy asked about my marriage before I moved on it. Fear of the unknown and shame of the known paralyzed me. One Saturday evening as I sat alone in my apartment, a wave of loneliness washed over me and took me back to Happy's office. I recalled the resolve that dissipated as soon as I walked out the door. Now, for the first time since then, I would have called Paula if I had her phone number. She had changed it shortly after I left, though, because I had tried to call once, a year after I arrived in Texas. I wouldn't have wanted to hear from me, either. I hadn't attempted to contact her since that one time.

Instead of searching for her new number, which I may or may not have found, I chose a route I considered less intrusive. I clicked on Facebook for the first time in my life and set up an account under my legal name. I didn't understand enough about Facebook searches at the time to realize that *Brandon Wade* was far less obscure than *Brandon Gull*. If Paula happened to search for me, I would be more difficult to find. I took a grainy selfie for my profile picture and became a Facebook lurker, posting no updates and requesting no friends. I just wanted a peek at my wife and kids' life post-Brandon if they had opened up their lives for public consumption.

It didn't surprise me when I found few traces of Paula online, but Lisa was a different story. Through her various social media, I followed hers and Paula's and David's lives for much longer than I intended. A month passed. Two. Six. In what seemed a blink of an eye, Lisa marked twenty years since her father abandoned the family in a moving Mother's Day post. Had she not written that post, I might have reached out—at least I convinced myself that was true. Instead, I retreated into lurk mode.

Before Happy asked about my family again, I pieced together bits and pieces of their lives without me. David started a lawn care company as a teenager and grew it like a pro—got that from his mother. Lisa killed it in the classroom—not sure where she got that—and earned some nice college scholarship money. Paula worked and took care of the kids. David joined the U.S. Army, and his sister and mother could not have taken more pride in it. Lisa got engaged to a nice-looking young man with a future. Paula finally made it to the beach. David paid for it.

My son, whom I've never met, took my place as the man of the house. I should have been there for this Jake guy to ask for my daughter's hand in marriage. I should have taught David to use power equipment, driven him to the recruiter's office and asked him grown-up man questions on the way. It should have been me who took Paula to the beach over twenty years earlier. I enjoyed her fascination with the sand and the water vicariously through Lisa's photos and videos. My guilt and shame gave way to joy for Paula and our children for what they had made of the awful circumstances I created. For me, guilt and shame turned to sadness for what I now realized I had lost. No, let me correct myself. I didn't *lose* my family; I gave it away. Part of my metamorphosis has been learning to call things what they are.

I longed to reach out to Paula. What would I say? Where would I start? *Hey, I realize it has been a while, but I saw where you finally went to the beach?* I couldn't do that to her, just pop in like I had gone on a business trip and lost my way home. No opening line, however contrite, expressed enough responsibility. The longer I waited, the more my flesh wanted to let her go. Her life was comfortable without me, and I had little to offer twenty years later. Lisa would hate me for complicating her wedding plans by reaching out at that point. As much as I longed to witness her big day, I had not earned the right. David would think I was reconnecting for a handout since he had accomplished more than I had in twice as many years. Happy was right about asking forgiveness and making reparations as much as I was able, but the timing wasn't right. Through God's forgiveness of me and Lisa's Facebook page, I came to love the family I had abandoned. Too much to insert myself into their existence.

A few days after I made the decision to remain distant until after Lisa's wedding, a familiar voice from the past called my name.

9

I was having a good day, too. Errands in the morning, Bible study with Jacob and Roger to preview our upcoming study of Jeremiah, and an easy Friday afternoon that ended with a light conversation with Happy. I was looking forward to grabbing a bite to eat and walking over to the stadium a few blocks over to watch a high school football game. Two teams shared the same stadium, so one of them played a home game every Friday night during the fall. With nothing else to do and not wanting to slip back into lazy habits, I attended all the games, enjoying the sport I had once played. One team was hosting a playoff game, and the weather on this November Friday night was perfect. With my mind on the game as I pulled into a parking spot outside my building, I didn't connect the voice to its source right away.

"Long day?"

"Yeah, it was," I answered before I turned to see who

asked, perhaps one of my neighbors with whom I exchanged occasional small talk. The front tag read Virginia, likely a rental. I saw her about the time the tone of her voice registered with my long-term memory. "Paula? No. Way. How did you find me? What are you doing here?" The accusing voice deep inside of me roared to life. *Dang it, Brandon, you should have made the move to apologize. Now, there's no way she'll believe you.*

"Yes. Yes way. You don't want to know. To forgive you and let go of the bitterness that I have carried since you left."

Hundreds of times since Happy pushed me to reconcile with Paula, I had run our meeting through my mind —what I would say and how she would respond. Not one of those scenarios included any sort of contrition on her part. She wanted to tell me she was sorry? Unbelievable. And amiss. She had done nothing wrong.

I realized I was standing without offering a word. Scrambling for a response, I tripped over my words and risked coming across standoffish. "Sure, yeah. Are you hoping to do that as quickly as possible, or would you mind sitting down and having a conversation?" *Please choose the latter. You've come so far. This may be my last chance.*

"A conversation, I think," she said, which I could imagine was not her reflexive answer. It was possible she viewed this as a last chance exchange like I did.

I risked letting her off the hook by asking if she could give me a few minutes to clean up and change clothes. After she agreed, I suggested, "We can go..."

Paula cut me off, snapping that she was not going

out for a drink with me. That felt foreign to me by then, but I reminded myself of the last me she knew. "I was going to suggest we grab a bite to eat. There's a fantastic Mexican place a mile from here."

Paula bit her lip in a way I recalled from when her emotions used to slip past her lips unchecked. She swallowed hard before she answered, "Sure, I'll wait."

"You sure?" She responded that she had brought a book to read, and I realized she had been casing my place for who knows how long.

I promised to hurry. I did, too, straight to my knees at one of my breakfast chairs, where I prayed every morning before heading to work. Each day, I prayed for Happy and Jacob and Roger and C.J. I lifted Paula and Lisa and David to God, asking Him to bless them with a relationship with Him if they weren't His already and for Him to use them if they did. I prayed for the courage to say I'm sorry and ask their forgiveness and for opportunity. I hadn't imagined the opportunity would come to me instead of my going to it. After a desperate prayer that lasted longer than intended, I threw on a clean pair of jeans, a Texas Rangers T-shirt, and a pair of sneakers. I slapped on some deodorant and ran some water through my hair before rushing back downstairs.

When I returned to the door of her rental, Paula asked, "Since when are you into football?" Twenty years earlier, I would have berated her for not knowing the difference between football and baseball teams. Not today. I couldn't blow this opportunity by reverting to my former self even one time.

"The Rangers are the baseball team here in Dallas.

Arlington, actually. I've been to some games with the Jacob and C.J. from work."

"Oh, right, football is the Cowboys, right?" *Whew, survived that correction. She seems embarrassed and extremely nervous.*

"Yeah. Believe it or not, I went to one of their games, too. I had to see that stadium that everybody's talking about. It's massive. Not that I can compare many sports stadiums to it, but I can't imagine one any bigger." *Listen to me rambling on about football stadiums.* I had discarded my plan to help fill the one whose lights filled the sky in the distance.

"Everything's bigger in Texas, right?" *Her attempts at small talk are about as awkward as mine.*

"So they say. Is Mexican okay with you?" She agreed.

I didn't want to add the ticklish choice of whether to ride together or in separate vehicles, so I gave her the address in case we became separated. During the few blocks' drive, I prayed. I was grateful for a quiet back corner table at 6:00 on a Friday night. Most folks in that part of town were tailgating at the game.

Paula seemed surprised when I ordered water with lemon, my drink of choice for long enough that I no longer craved beer.

Earlier, when I had rushed to my apartment for an impromptu prayer, I sensed God giving me strength to face what I had coming to me. Now, I stared across the table at my ex-wife, whom I hadn't seen in two decades. She was as attractive as ever, but I chalked it up to not having a date since I left her. I labeled her "nervously relaxed," like she had made quite an effort to look like she didn't make much of an effort. *You think this is a date, you bozo? Get ahold of yourself. She's about to blast you, and you're going to sit here and take it like the man you never were for her.*

"So, Paula, I'm sure you didn't come out here for chitchat, so I'll skip the *you're looking great* banter. Where did you want to start?" *Well, that came across as brusque. Soften the blow, why don't you?* I called myself a bozo again.

"Brandon, you hurt me when you left, and you took all our money. It has been a hard life, providing for two kids and trying to give them a chance in life. I lost my job because of you, which put us in a hole and threatened to send us onto the government dole." *Ouch. Twenty years of anger packed into a lead right cross that hurt more than the one Stearns had landed on my face years earlier.* "But it didn't. You never once reached out about your two children." *Body blow.* "Honestly, I preferred it that way." *Right uppercut square on the jaw.* "But I have come to recognize the depth of the bitterness I held toward what you did to us, and I understand the only way to turn it loose is to forgive you. You don't owe me any explanations or money or future contact or even an apology. I need to do this for me. So, bottom line, Brandon, while your leaving hurt me and hurt our children, I forgive you, no strings attached."

Paula's words stunned me, but not from her pinpoint shots to the places I felt the deepest shame. About that time, our server arrived to take our orders, but—praise God—she recognized we were having a moment and didn't interrupt. I mouthed *thank you* to her and turned my attention back to my vulnerable wife. *Does she still consider herself your wife? I mean, that's where this is ultimately going, that she wants to make things official with a divorce so she can move on, right? Geez, man, don't leave her sitting there—say something!*

"Paula, that was brave. Thank you. That was my responsibility—asking your forgiveness, that is." *Careful, Brandon, don't hijack her apology.* "I wanted to say I'm sorry, but by the time I came around to understanding the depth of what I had done, I was too ashamed to reach out. I've been trying to work my way toward reaching out for the last few months." *She's still listening. You owe her an explanation.* "My bad habits followed me out here and only got worse. I got in some trouble a few months after I got here..." Paula's tiniest flinch answered one of my unspoken questions. "That's how you found me."

She confessed.

"Then you understand the mess I made of my first ten years here." She nodded. "There was a considerable sum of illicit money the police didn't find under a trap door in that house. When the couple I was staying with went to jail, I took it. I'm not proud of what I did, and I paid for it later. All the while knowing they'd come looking for their money when they got out of prison, I still burned through almost all of it. I could have just moved, tried to start over new somewhere else, but I was stupid and fast running out of money, so I stayed. After they confronted me, let's just say I started a business to repay the money. Sales and distribution."

"You started dealing drugs."

"Yeah. Like I said, it's not something I'm proud of, but I'm giving you the unvarnished truth. I almost got busted when the cops arrested me for trespassing at the school near my apartment. One of their principals was watching me, so I walked halfway around the track and then to the bathroom behind the baseball field to get out of his sight. I hid the drugs where nobody would find them and came back to the track, where the cops arrested me. The charges didn't stick, but I wanted no more of the drug-selling lifestyle. I had paid the guy back everything I owed him, so I told him I quit." *I'll spare her the specifics of the laziness that defined the years between our last interaction and now.* "Promise," I said, raising my right hand, "I haven't dealt or used drugs since." *I never used except for a handful of times, but she won't believe that.*

Our server returned to take our orders, and I fast-forwarded to meeting Happy. "I started going to this recovery group, and the guy who leads it owns an electrical company. He believed me when I told him I was looking to make a fresh start. Since he has taken chances on a lot of guys in recovery and gotten burned a few times, I knew what a risk he was taking. He started me on the paperwork the next week before my drug test, which I knew I would pass. I didn't make much money when I started, but he gave me all the overtime I wanted and, just today, a company truck so I wouldn't depend on co-workers to get to work."

If Paula had studied the court transcripts, she might recognize some inconsistencies in my story now. "I wasn't lying to that judge, by the way—I sold my boat and my truck, though not in the manner I told him." *That seemed random. Where am I going with this? Get back on track.* "Sometimes overtime meant cleaning up around the shop, but I paid my bills and put back some cash for a house in a better part of town and something of my own to drive. Once I could buy a car, I was planning to come back to Mississippi to find you and apologize for all I've done. Step nine of recovery is to make amends as much as possible. There's no way I could go back and change things with you or with Lisa and David, but I could help in the future, perhaps with Lisa's wedding. She doesn't need to know."

"How did you know about her engagement?" *Is this a test or does she know I've been stalking them? Honesty, fella —this conversation better drip it, or you can write off your family forever.*

"Facebook. I guess I'm what you call a lurker."

She waited for what seemed like forever before she responded. I recognized that though I no longer carried the trappings of a seedier member of society, she had every right to view me that way. At last, she held out her hand. "Give me your phone." I resisted the urge to ask why, instead passing it across the table without comment.

"Smile," she said, snapping a photo as soon as I did. "Now go update that atrocious profile pic of yours." *She knows. She didn't snap. Did I notice the tiniest hint of a smile?*

"So I'm not the only Facebook lurker?"

"Just trying to find you. Probably better I didn't find

a phone number for you, or I might have just called instead of drumming up the courage to come out here to face you myself." *Courage? Why would it take courage to confront me?*

Fumbling for what to say next, I offered, "I'm glad you're here. I wish this would have been me coming to Mississippi years ago."

"I would've knocked you all the way back to Texas." There was the Paula I expected if we ever met again, a flash of fire in her eyes that extinguished almost immediately.

"I would have deserved it, too. Paula, I am truly sorry for everything I put you and Lisa and David through. I sometimes think back and wonder if it could have worked out differently. There's one thing in particular I wish I could do over. The night that you told me you were pregnant for the first time, we talked about... do you remember?"

"We talked about going to church the next morning."

"You remember. My brain was so foggy back then and for years afterward, but I remember that night clearly. I was ready to change everything for our baby, and I knew God and church were the places to start, but then I just... didn't. I've tried to figure out why. In case you ever wondered what was real and what wasn't, that intention was one hundred percent real. But when I laid my head down that night, my inner voice asked me who I thought I was fooling. I wonder how things might have played out differently. We might have followed God's plan for marriage and parenting. We might have made new friends. I might have stopped drinking. I might have kept my job, and you obviously would have kept yours."

"Guess we'll never know." *Had understanding stepped in where bitterness used to be in Paula?*

"No, I reckon not." Those were some of the saddest words ever to leave my mouth. As I stared across the table at the physical representation of what I had thrown away in my life, I wondered if Paula felt the same. Our food arrived, and the moment passed.

10

As Paula and I ate, a question welled up inside of me that I hoped wouldn't be out of bounds. When I couldn't stand the silence any longer, I straightened and said, "Would you mind telling me about Lisa and David? If you don't want to, I'll understand." I made sure not to claim any part of their lives.

Paula took a while to finish her brisket taco, a solid choice for a first-timer at Del Norte. I feared she would cut the conversation short, but she wiped the corner of her mouth and asked what I knew about them.

"Not much except through Lisa's Facebook page. David seems pretty private, at least online. I saw Lisa is about to graduate college and get married, all in one day. I hope her day is everything she desires it to be. From her posts, I put together that David served our country in the army and that he is quite the young entrepreneur. I know he is generous with his money."

Oh, crap. I'll never recover from that. Stupid Brandon.

Pay attention to her face. That's exactly how she took it. Might as well prepare to say goodbye. No, dadgummit, that's not what I meant.

"No, Paula, no, I wouldn't dare," I scrambled. "I was talking about your beach trip, Lisa's engagement and all."

"Oh, sorry." *Is she going to stay? Boy, she sure has changed. But why shouldn't she? You've changed, too, though. Let her see it.*

I hung my head and told her she had every right. "I was just going to say I'm glad you finally got your beach trip. You've earned it. Lisa and David seem like wonderful people. You did good, Paula." That sounded hollow.

"Thanks." *Did she just smile? She did, no doubt about it. Lord, I've been praying for this, so I shouldn't be surprised that You're answering, but You are and I am.*

Paula thought for another moment before she spoke with less edginess in her tone. "Lisa is quiet and thoughtful, smart. She paid her way through college with scholarships and part-time jobs, studied hard, and met the man she's going to marry. What could be better, right? Jake's a keeper, too. We love him. For him to have enough consideration for our family to include us—especially David while he was in Iraq—in his proposal to Lisa was beyond special for all of us. I enjoyed getting to know his family, too. I was a little nervous before our trip, but they're good people, normal folks. Lisa has earned everything that's come her way, and I couldn't be prouder of her or happier for her.

"David didn't do as well in school because he found

his interest in his yard cutting business. I tell you what, that fit him like a glove. He works hard and takes a lot of pride in the work he does. His customers love him, but I tell you what convinced me he had found his passion was when he started hiring people. He didn't wait until he needed help and then hire the first one of his friends to step forward. No, he developed quite a vetting process before he hired his first helper at sixteen. The kids—I call them kids, but *young men* would be a better term—who ran his business while he was gone were mirror images of David. To me, that was a testament to how he trained them. He pays them well and expects them to deliver the best customer service of anybody in the business.

"He could have finished high school and made fine money right off the bat if he had wanted to cut yards full time. It wouldn't have been a problem for him to expand. Brandon, he had a waiting list of people who wanted to hire him when he left for basic training. That's unheard of. Anyway, he loves our country and wanted to serve a tour of duty in the army. He did his three years, saved almost everything he made, and now he's ready to go to college to get a business degree to go along with the business he already has. His plan is to expand gradually until he's finished with college and then devote all his time to it or start another business."

I listened intently as Paula bragged on both children, but I couldn't help but notice when she called me by name. *How long before she comes to her senses about sharing such personal reflections with me after all I had done… and not done.* When she paused, I used the opportunity to say, "I'm glad neither one of them turned out like me." I must have said it more to myself because Paula asked me to repeat it. When I did, I felt a tear rolling down my cheek. I snatched it away, but she had noticed. *What in the world is going on? What right do I have to bemoan my circumstances in front of Paula? At least it will give her some satisfaction to make me cry.*

"I'll be honest with you, that has been one of my biggest fears all these years." *Here it comes. Time to pile on and then split.* "Brandon, look, I'm not looking to pile on." *Is she reading my mind?* "I can tell you have regrets. Until recently, that was what I wanted. But last year I met a group of folks unexpectedly, and they said some things that made me reflect on life and myself. One guy in the group had a meltdown on his way to the restaurant where we all met. It was years in the making, but to the rest of us listening to his story, it seemed inevitable. When I thought about the anger, bitterness, and defensiveness I've been carrying for far longer than he had, I recognized that if I didn't deal with it soon, the next meltdown would be mine."

Stunned doesn't even begin to describe my reaction to Paula's story. Right there in front of me, I had witnessed her countenance shift away between who she had been and who she was becoming. I wondered if she could sense the change in me through my expressions. I doubted it. *Listen, stupid. She's pouring her heart out to you, of all people. The least you could do is pay attention.*

"There was a pastor in our group," Paula continued, "whose wife was murdered by a homeless man she was trying to help. The way he described his wife, she seemed like an angel, the type person that everybody loves. She gave her time and energy to all kinds of people. For her to be shot down after serving God by feeding the guy who shot her later—it seemed the most despicable thing one human being could do to another. And yet, this pastor was telling her story all calm and composed, and it was his first Thanksgiving without her. I was angry, I'll tell you. Angry. Angry at the man who killed her. And, frankly, angry at the pastor for not being angry with him. He forgave him instead, even took a Thanksgiving meal to the jail for him that day. Who does that, right?" *She used the word* angry *several times in a row, and she didn't aim one of them in your direction. Female companionship is nice, isn't it? Pay attention!*

"As I told my story, I realized I had far less to be angry about than he did. When those folks started telling me what an exceptional mother I had been, I didn't believe them. Then, they started pointing out character qualities they saw in my kids through the stories I told about them. It was like I was so focused on keeping food on the table and on my fear that they would take a sudden right turn like..."

Here it was, all that anger pinpointed in my direction. I didn't notice when Paula stopped at first, but in the silence, my mind fast-forwarded to where she stopped.

"Like their old man?" I asked.

"Actually, I was going to say *like their mother*. I'd never put it together before, but I had great parents, two super parents. They gave me everything I needed and a lot of what I wanted, but that was never enough for me.

All they asked in return was respect. When I turned sixteen, I decided I wouldn't give it to them anymore, that I wanted to make my own way in the world. Brandon, all this time, I thought I was afraid they would turn out like you, but it was me I was more afraid they would follow. I'm sorry." *Wait, what just happened? Did she just blame her frustration on herself? It's not her fault. You've got to say something. Look at her. She's make herself vulnerable to you. This is the miracle you've prayed for times a thousand. Say something.*

"You didn't want them turning out like me, either," I answered at last. This was my chance to say the words I had rehearsed but had fallen flat at every recitation. "I had my own way until I choked on it. You would think there wouldn't be anybody who would look out for my best interests than me, but when I've tried to control my own life, I've steered it in the ditch every time. Paula, the truth is, when I left, I wasn't leaving you and our kids as much as I was running from myself. I'm not making excuses—what I did was wrong and without excuse—but the weight of the responsibility that I was about to have... a son, my family name... the pressure overwhelmed me. I convinced myself that both of our kids would be better off never remembering me. It was a coward's way out. I was wrong and I'm sorry. By the time I turned my life around—rather, by the time God changed me—I had no right in your lives. I know that, and you won't ever have to worry about me trying to show up where I'm not wanted."

There, I had said it. Years of regret poured out across a red-and-white checked tablecloth, two half-finished plates, and two glasses nervously emptied. The words had flowed this time. I breathed a long sigh of relief, my greatest burden shared with the person least likely to agree to carry it.

"Brandon, I..." *No, don't let her start a war of greater fault. Stop her now!*

"Wait, don't respond to that," I said, now past the rehearsed apology. "I'm not looking to push you toward anything. I realize you came out here to release me from anything I owe you, and I totally respect and admire that. The last thing I desire is to complicate things, so let's leave it here, okay? I accept your forgiveness, even if I don't think you have anything to be forgiven. Let me repeat that I was wrong to leave, more wrong to steal what was more yours than mine, and even more wrong to leave you to raise what should have been our children."

I could no longer hide my tears, which had a mind of their own. Through my blurred vision, I could have sworn I noticed her swallowing hard to hold back her own tears. "Paula, let me say, though, that you have been—you are—an amazing mother. I'm glad you found a group of people to tell you that. You deserve it. Lisa and David are a testament to how hard you've worked to give them a life they never would have had if I had stayed. One thing I would ask you to consider, maybe on your drive back to Mississippi: Would you think about forgiving me for what I have done to you and to Lisa and David? If there's any kind of restitution I could make, you just name it."

"Brandon, I—"

I stopped her again. "Don't answer now. Think on it."

Paula forced her way over my objection. "Brandon, I don't have to. I forgive you. I'm not starting that cycle of unforgiveness over again. You don't owe us a thing."

11

Paula drove back to her hotel in Garland thirty minutes after our exchange of apologies. In between we chatted as old acquaintances with a common past still linked by two children and a piece of paper with notarized signatures that she never mentioned. She drove back to Mississippi the next morning, and a tsunami of sadness rolled over me. For the better part of Saturday morning, I poured my heart out to God, asking Him to help me sort out the myriad feelings washing over me. Around noon it occurred to me that Happy wasn't aware of what had happened in the last sixteen hours.

"Happy, please tell me you have some free time right now. If you don't, I just might burst."

"Easy, cowboy, just so happens I crossed off the last

item from my honey-do list a few minutes ago. You had lunch yet?"

"Lunch, no." I sensed elation from my mid-section and realized I had forgotten to eat breakfast.

"I'll meet you at Whataburger in fifteen minutes."

Our back sides had barely hit the chairs when I blurted, "You'll never guess what happened, Happy."

"Tell you what. Let's say a blessing over our food first, and I'll take a stab at it." Happy removed his company cap and said a quick prayer. As soon as he said *amen*, he grinned and said, "You finally called her, didn't you?"

"Better." That piqued his interest. Relating the events of the previous evening and the various emotions pestering me since, I summarized, "I'm relieved I said the words I've rehearsed so long and ecstatic that she accepted my apology. I'm ashamed she initiated the conversation by driving all the way out here when I should have started it, but she forgave me, Happy. I'm still a little confused why she would feel she owed me forgiveness. Maybe *owed* isn't the best word."

"Yeah, if you owe someone forgiveness, is it truly forgiveness? Perhaps she felt *compelled* instead of *obligated*."

"That's better. With the dishes cleared and apologies done, Paula and I talked like we never did back in the day. It was easy, not quite like talking to you but certainly not as awkward as the beginning of the conversation."

"Almost like God was controlling the conversation from both sides?"

"More like *guiding*, but, yeah."

"How did you feel when you looked at her?"

"What do you mean?"

"Was she attractive to you?"

"I didn't focus on that, honest. Happy, she gave her life to the Lord last year. Even though I haven't been a part of her life for the last twenty years, I can tell He's changing her. Every time she would catch herself responding as she would have in the past, it was like the Lord reached out and redirected her."

"Could be that she has been praying about talking to you as much as you've been praying about talking to her."

"I hadn't considered that, but you're probably right. There were times I knew the Lord was directing my words. We could have gotten off track if the first words hadn't been full of contrition for either of us."

Happy leaned back and took a sip of his sweet tea. "So, Brandon, I'll ask you again: Were you attracted to her?"

It wasn't like Happy to fixate on something so surface.

"I confess she looked better across the table than you do."

"You don't want to answer the question, Brandon, but that's okay. Your neck says it for you." *Stupid neck. Why does it have to turn red every time I'm embarrassed to speak? And why did Happy have to notice that early in our friendship?*

"It keeps me honest," I answered, as much to my inner voice as to his.

"Did you get her number?"

"What are we, fifteen? What gives?"

"Brandon, I'm going to reveal something I believe the Lord showed me some time ago in our relationship. You were still walking through the fog of years of poor decisions, and it would have only confused you to mention it, so I've kept it to myself. Did you ever wonder why I insisted you attend recovery group with me, even though you swore you weren't addicted to drugs?"

"I wasn't."

"I understand, but the point is you still needed recovery. You needed help to break a cycle of hurts, hang-ups, and habits."

I smiled at the mention of a part of the group's mantra. "Do you remember the message you were putting on the church sign the day we met?"

"I believe it said, 'Looking for a way to escape your rut?'"

"Yeah, well, that wasn't the first time I had seen you pose that question on your sign."

"No?"

I confessed to reading Happy's sign and being drawn to it months before we connected, only to be sucked back into my unproductive lifestyle that lasted until I read the same words again.

He shook his head. "Do you realize I make it a point not to post the same message on that sign twice? I made an exception that once because I sensed someone needed to see it. That's the day I met you, but I couldn't have known you had been marinating in that message for so long. But God knew. I had prepared another saying for the church sign that week, but the Lord knew what you needed to read."

"Do you remember the other message?"

"Yeah, it was 'A rut is nothing but a grave with the ends kicked out.'"

"Truth."

"Yeah, but too crafty and a bit harsh—too condescending for my taste. I'm glad I chose the old one."

"I'd like to imagine that it wouldn't have mattered, and I would have approached you, anyway."

"Just as I hope you would have contacted Paula at some point."

"About that—I felt ashamed after we sat down, and she apologized first. It worked out fine, and I said all the things I needed to say, but I should have initiated it."

"You're right, but you can stop beating yourself up over it now. What's done is done, and the Lord answered our prayers."

"Pressed down, shaken together, and running over."

"For sure. You ready?"

I stood and emptied my tray before walking by the counter and thanking the workers for fixing lunch, as Happy had taught me to do. Just before I ducked my head inside my truck, I looked over at Happy and grinned.

"Yeah," I said.

"Yeah, what?"

"She gave me her number."

I TEXTED Paula's number the day after she returned to Mississippi, thanking her again for forgiving my offenses against her and our children. I dared not ask anything in return. Because of the emotion of our Friday night conversation, I wondered if her mind would clear on her drive back and give her second thoughts about wiping the slate clean with me. She sent a brief text in return: *The Lord has done a magnificent work in me and in you, too. Grateful.* That was it. No emojis, no caps, no exclamation points to hint at her emotions two days after seeing me for the first time in twenty years.

A thousand times over the next few days, I picked up my phone to text her again, maybe even to dial her number. Each time, though, I returned the phone to my pocket. The voice in my head convinced me to wait, that the next move should be hers. I argued that part of gaining control of my life was rejecting the passivity that had plagued me for so long. But my fingers would not follow through.

On the Friday night after Thanksgiving, I was just about to walk out the door to give my testimony of restoration at recovery group when my phone buzzed in my pocket. When I pulled it out and recognized the caller as Paula Gull, two thoughts hit me simultaneously. One was how my heart shot into my throat like a seventh-grade boy getting a call back from the girl he wants to ask to the middle school dance. The other was that she had kept my last name longer than I had. Changing my name seemed silly at that moment.

"You busy?"

"On my way to recovery group but I'll make time."

"No, no, no—don't miss on account of me."

"Can I call you later when I get out? I wasn't planning on staying after the large group meeting tonight, but I'm speaking in it, so I kind of have to be there."

"Understood. Call me back if it's not too late."

"Eight-thirty at the latest. I promise." Ouch. *You might not ought to use that word with Paula. Just saying.*

"That's fine."

"Paula, is everything okay?"

"Yeah. You remember the Thanksgiving group I told you about when I was in Texas?"

"Yeah, Lonesome, party of something-or other."

"Six. Well, we met for our reunion last night, and some stuff came up that I thought we might discuss."

My heart sank. *Here comes the divorce request. She couldn't bring herself to ask in person. Doesn't matter. Give it to her. It's the least you can do after twenty years without a word.* I drew from every ounce of goodwill I had toward Paula and said goodbye until later.

My heart was heavy as I sat at a table with Happy and four of the other regulars, moving food around my plate but not finding any of it appetizing. Happy noticed. I chalked it up to being nervous about speaking later, and if he doubted me, he didn't say. By the time I was to stand and tell my story of forgiveness and making amends, the anxiousness was real. The hopeful tone I had rehearsed throughout the week gave way to a more doleful appeal to follow the steps toward freedom. My words contained the truth that the people in the room needed to work out, but I could no longer offer the bow on top of the gift of release from regret. My inner voice reminded me at every turn that sin has consequences. The clock was ticking ever closer to eight.

At 8:05, I prayed for the group gathered in the church's fellowship hall and slipped out a side door while Happy transitioned the meeting into smaller groups. He would think me rude for not sticking around, but he would have mercy when I explained my day of reckoning. My conversation with Paula might be short enough that I could catch Happy in the parking lot before he left and empty my sorrows to him. I sensed I would require his support before the night was over.

I poked along on the drive home. At 8:15, I pulled into a convenience store for a comfort candy bar and a bottled sweet tea. My knotted stomach rejected the idea, and I left with neither. My inner voice convinced me to quit procrastinating and make the call. I drove home, dropped my keys on the counter, and settled into my sunken spot on the couch, and tapped out Paula's number at 8:27.

"HEY, there. I was wondering if you were going to call. How did your talk go?" Paula sounded upbeat, but I was in no mood for small talk.

"Fine, I guess."

"What did you talk about?"

"Forgiveness and making amends."

"So you talked about our meeting?" It didn't seem like an accusation.

"Nothing too specific, but yeah."

"Were you nervous, standing in front of people and being so transparent before them? I have gotten so good at wearing a mask that I'm not sure who the real me is anymore. Except my Lonesome party of six friends—I feel like I can be myself with them."

Empathy. I had found it through Happy and Jacob, and it's what the collection of broken people gaping at me an hour earlier had needed more than my words. I hadn't given it to them, but Paula was giving it to me. *Before the other shoe drops.*

"Brandon?"

"Uh, yeah, I was... I'm sorry, what was the question?"

"I asked if you were nervous."

"I suppose I was. I've spoken at recovery group before and not been apprehensive, but this time was different." *A reason I suppose you'll reveal when you're good and ready.*

"Why do you think that was?"

Might as well get to it now. "You said you had something to discuss with me. I was thinking about that, so I was distracted." *Oh, so you're blaming her.* "Don't hear that I'm blaming you. My mind just couldn't help wandering."

"Oh, I'm sorry I caught you when I did. It could have waited."

"Paula, I should have asked your permission before sharing my story with the group tonight. That was wrong and I'm sorry."

Silence.

"Paula?"

"I'm here."

"What's wrong?"

"I shared our story, too. It never crossed my mind that I should have talked to you first. Separate ways, worlds apart, and everything." I smiled on my end of the phone when she quoted one of the song lyrics we sang together during some of our rare happier times. "Brandon, I'm sorry." *Is she crying?*

"It's okay. You're right, we live in such different worlds that the people we shared our stories with are not likely to cross paths."

Silence.

"Paula?"

"I'm here."

"You okay?"

"No."

"What's wrong?"

"That's not exactly true."

"What's not?"

"That the people with whom we shared our stories are not likely to cross paths."

"What do you mean?"

"Brandon, this is why I called you. Oh my gosh, this is so much harder than I thought it would be."

The empathy I should have shown at recovery group showed itself at that moment. "Paula, if you're calling to ask for a divorce, I won't stand in your way. I'll pay…"

"No," she interrupted. "That's not it at all… wait, is that why you were so nervous tonight?"

"Well, yeah," I confessed. "That's not what you wanted…?" My outer voice trailed off as my inner voice roared to life. *You two really must work on your communication skills. That's been an issue from the beginning, so if you're going to move toward your kids, you'd better get used to being transparent with her.*

"Would it help if I said I was nervous about this conversation, too?"

"Yes, but if I can add something without offending you, it would be more helpful if you'd just say what you called to say." *That sounded rude.* "Sorry, that sounded rude."

"We should trademark this apology dance we've been doing. Okay, okay, here goes. Last night was my reunion with Lonesome, party of six. Everybody brought family and friends, and we met the young lady who noticed us and bought our supper last year. Each one of our group told an amazing story of how God has worked over the past year. Brandon, it was overwhelming. The pastor who led me to the Lord—remember I told you his wife had been murdered—well, his best friend passed away, and the Lord brought him and his friend's wife together. I know that sounds straight from a tabloid talk show, but if you had heard him tell his story—well, the Lord has been at work in both of them. I won't bore you with all the stories that won't mean much to you, but understand this is the first group of people I've opened up to since you left. They're the reason I dealt with my bitterness and guilt… sorry, I'm rambling."

"It's okay. Whatever it took to bring you to freedom… believe me, I'm interested."

"When it came my turn, I was so overwhelmed with

the stories the others before me had told, I didn't hold back. I told them about our beach trip and Lisa's engagement and David's homecoming. And I told them about my trip to Texas, all of it. Brandon, I have to tell you again that I didn't consider asking you first, and I'm sorry, but I didn't go to the reunion planning to share it."

"It's okay."

"What I didn't consider when I told it was that Lisa and David were sitting right there. I got so caught up in the moment of sharing with my friends that I didn't consider that I hadn't told them about coming to Texas yet."

My heart sank.

12

"Brandon?"

"I'm still here."

"Okay, didn't hear you for a sec and thought I might have lost you." I wondered if she captured the irony of her words. "So when I finished telling the group about what happened out there, I noticed Lisa close to tears and hanging on the Jake with one hand and David with the other. Her voice was shaky when she asked how we left it."

"Left what?"

"Our standing with one another. I told her we left with a clean slate, that we wiped away many years of regret, some we didn't even realize we had. I assured her you seemed different. One girl in our Lonesome group is working through the recovery steps, and she had a tough time with forgiveness and restitution, too. We had already listened to her story, which is one reason I felt so free to share my journey."

"How did Lisa respond?"

"I didn't paint you out to be a bad guy, Brandon. I tried not to do that while the kids were growing up, but their teenage curiosity led to a lot of questions. My answers were honest, but they may have also stirred up the bitterness toward you that weighed heavier as the kids moved closer toward high school and graduation and the real world beyond it."

"Paula, I…"

"Brandon, don't. You're forgiven. I'm not piling on, just setting up what happened next last night."

"Okay, go ahead."

"I wanted Lisa and David to understand I'm no longer wallowing in my bitterness and that I didn't come to see you for any other reason. I was honest with them about my defenses reminding me of bad roads I've traveled by taking you at your word."

"I've earned that." *But it still hurts to hear you say it out loud.*

"I told them the positive, too, about your job and your promotion and company truck and all. I admit I called your apartment a dump—at least from the outside—and I could have kept that to myself. The context was your saving to buy a house and my hope that you could."

"It's all right. This place *is* a dump, and I've thrown rent money at it far too long. It's what I can afford for now, but that should change soon."

"All that to say that Lisa started to ask me a question. She said, 'Mom, do you think…' and then she trailed off and suggested we discuss it after the party.

Again, caught up in the moment, I gave her permission to ask in front of everybody. Emotion overcame her, so David finished the question for her: '… that he would want a relationship with us?'"

"Are you serious?"

"His exact words."

"Forgive me if I didn't see that coming."

"Me, either. Over these past two decades, I kept one focus: taking care of Lisa and David. I didn't cultivate friendships, I didn't date, and I neglected my personal care on their behalf. What I observed last night was that my kids needed a daddy. Now, before you go two-stepping with that apology dance we've become so adept at, hear me out. Their response was a gut shot to me, but not like you might imagine. It humbled me—and that's putting it lightly—that I had been less than everything they needed. God had to walk me through that during my time with Him this morning, to remind me that if I had been everything they needed, they wouldn't have a need for Him."

I hated to interrupt while Paula shared such personal thoughts, so I forced myself to wait. My mind was whirring with how she answered our children. When she paused, I asked, "What did you tell them?"

"That I kept my coming to Texas from them because releasing you was something *I* needed to do. I didn't consider how things might progress from there. My Facebook lurking didn't lead me to expect God had changed your life like He has. Your new profile pic is a solid improvement, by the way."

"It'll do until I go for my glamour shots."

"Oh, my gosh, you still remember that?"

"You talked about it only slightly less than going to the beach."

"Guilty. That seems so silly now, especially for a girl stuck in the trucking industry. Back then, though, doing a glamour photo shoot seemed like the ultimate pampering."

"Besides a week at the beach."

"I'm glad there's no evidence of my big hair days—no glamour shots or even yearbook photos for my kids to tease me about relentlessly."

"I miss your big hair. When you called out to me from your car, your voice was familiar, but it took me a minute to reconcile the voice with your hair. It fits you, though."

"Thanks. All right, back on track. David said, 'He is our father. I've never met him, and Lisa doesn't remember him at all. I think I speak for both of us that we don't want to make you uncomfortable because you're our mom, and you've been the one who has poured yourself into us all these years. But if he has changed like you say, maybe it's time?'"

Paula recollected David's words in a matter-of-fact manner as I shook and fought in vain to remain composed. Happy had taught me we sometimes pray outlandish prayers that God doesn't seem to hear. He pushed me to pray for reconciliation to Paula, which seemed the outer limits of God's capacity to work in my broken life. Happy wouldn't allow me to stop there, though. "How big do you think God is?" he often asked before we dove into a Bible passage together. I see now that he challenged my faith to grow by leading me to stories where people had the audacity to ask Jesus to heal them of lifelong conditions, even ask Him to raise someone from the dead. Since being restored to my children fell short of that, dropping it into the realm of possibility, I prayed God would bring me back to them. At the end of most of those prayers, like the man who asked Jesus to deliver his son from demons, I would add "Lord, I believe. Help my unbelief."

When Paula called and wanted to talk, my narrow view of God told me to have a positive attitude about granting her a divorce. I delayed the call as long as possible and then expected the worst. Now, she was telling me that our children desired a relationship with the father who had long ago abandoned them. Paula gave me a moment to collect myself. My unbelief was taking a shellacking.

"And Lisa?" I finally managed.

"Her, too." Paula waited a moment longer before asking if I was sitting.

"Yeah, I'm sitting. Why?"

"Lisa was shaking with emotion, so I wanted to shut down the public discussion of what I should have presented to them in private. I told her and David that I would call you soon to see if you were ready to meet them."

"Sure, I…"

"Hold on, there's more. Brace yourself. Lisa asked if there was a chance you might attend her wedding." *Stop it, Lord. I'm overwhelmed.* "I asked if she was sure she wanted you there."

"And she said *yes*?"

"Here's what she said: 'No. And yes. What I mean is, I don't want him to be there because of any part he has played in my life. I still want David to walk me down the aisle and you to stand with me as my maid of honor. Even though those are weird roles for y'all to be playing, it fits who we are as a family. But, if we have any type of relationship with Dad in the future, I want to be able to look back and remember that he was at least present at my wedding.'"

"Whoa." I was thankful Paula had instructed me to sit. My mind whirred with the possibility of attending my daughter's wedding in any capacity. She and her mother both had the right to nix any attempt on my behalf to reconnect, but the Lord was opening doors so fast that my limited mind couldn't comprehend. "She said that?"

"I instructed her to discuss it in private with Jake. Same with David and me. She never has been one to drag her feet to care of something important, so she talked to Jake last night. When I woke up and walked into the kitchen this morning, she and David were waiting for me. She hadn't backed up an inch, and neither had David."

"Tell her it would honor me to park cars at her wedding if I could watch it, even from a distance. And please inform her I won't do anything stupid to ruin her special day."

Paula laughed on the other end of the line, an easy laugh I remembered through the fog of twenty years.

"What kind of idiot do you think I've presented you to be?"

"The truth is sufficient."

"Brandon, just meet the kids and be as humble as you were when I came to Texas. Tell me you were genuine then."

"I would love to say *trust me, Paula, that's who I am now*. But when I consider those words moving from my heart to my mouth, I understand how shallow they must seem. If you give me this chance to prove myself, I hope you will see it's true."

Paula's tone turned serious. "Brandon, can I ask you something?"

"Anything."

"You're stumbling all over your bad choices from the past, aren't you? Like freedom isn't really free?"

I sat without a word for a solid minute. Paula waited. Any answer I formed in my mind fell short of representing the man I desired to be. I breathed a quick prayer and hoped for a quick response. *Answer the question like you're talking to Happy. You always give him the unadulterated truth. She's moving toward you. Accept that.*

"Paula, I'm going to shoot you straight. Except two or three times when I felt I had no choice, I never used drugs. I realize how insane it sounds for a clearheaded guy to deal drugs, but it's true. Even so, when Happy led me to the Lord, he insisted I start a recovery program. Since addicts lie to cover up their habits, I'm not sure he trusted what I told him about the drug use, or lack thereof. Still, recovery has served me well. My good intentions turned into small positive steps and then more significant ones. I would have labeled myself *recovered*."

"Until?"

"Until I had to answer a ghost from my past."

"Is that what I am?"

"Not you. Me. When I told Happy the unvarnished truth about my past, he zeroed in on the Paula part of it. He pushed me hard to ask your forgiveness and make amends. When I pushed back against it because it seemed like too much, too fast, he backed off but insisted I give it to the Lord. Paula, I have prayed long and hard for reconciliation with you and the kids."

When I stopped, she nudged. "But…?"

I ignored the question. "When you showed up here, the Lord answered my prayers so fast that I have been walking around in a daze ever since. And today, wow, I'm having a hard time processing it all."

"You're not telling me something."

Happy once taught me that if I was holding on to something I didn't want to tell him but needed to, I should count down *three, two, one,* and spit it out right then. I counted down and jerked up the roots. "Paula, it was when I started recovery that I went to work for Happy. He placed me with this guy named Jacob, who mentored me, taught me to study the Scriptures, how to pray—all the day-to-day elements of a walk with God. It was a brand spanking new life for me, and I loved every minute. I experienced the freedom from my hang-ups of the past… as long as I stayed in Richardson, Texas. Well before you showed up at my apartment complex, I recognized I wouldn't be truly free until I made my best attempt to reconcile with you and Lisa and David."

"What held you back?"

"I accepted what Jesus did for me on the cross. I accepted what Happy and Jacob were willing to do for me. But I couldn't forgive myself for abandoning you with two babies. My children. It's such an egregious sin that I couldn't imagine the Lord forgiving me for it, even though it happened before I gave my life to Him. I let it freeze me from doing the right thing. I'm glad you moved toward me, and I'm blown away that Lisa and David want to meet me. But…"

"Brandon, stop. You're headed down a dangerous road."

"What do you mean?"

"Do you believe I have forgiven you?"

"I'd sure like to hope so."

"I have. Do you trust that God has forgiven you?"

"Yes."

"And I told you Lisa and David want to move toward a relationship with you. That's forgiveness. Don't you see? If you have accepted their forgiveness and my forgiveness and God's forgiveness, what makes forgiving yourself more important? That's pride. Who even invented the idea of forgiving yourself, anyway? Even as a newcomer to the Bible, I'm pretty sure it's not in there."

"I never considered it like that. I may be a little further down the Bible study road, but I've never come across forgiving yourself, either. What makes you so smart?"

"Oh, don't assume *I* figured this out. I'm a high school dropout, remember? I told you one of my Lonesome, party of six friends is a pastor. His name is Calvin Hobbs, and..."

"Like the comic strip?"

Paula chuckled. "It was part of his introduction to the group. Anyway, he led me to the Lord, and he's a wonderful counselor. He asks a question or two and then sits back and lets you talk yourself into whatever you already realize you should do. I talk until I pin myself in a corner. When I reach that point, I realize I need to say out loud what I already understand to be right. Doing whatever the thing is becomes easier when I've said it out loud."

"Happy has a way of doing that."

"If you were working this out with him instead of me, what would you tell him?"

"That I can grab hold of my new life in Christ here where I made the change. Where I'm having a more troublesome time is making amends with the past. Something like that."

"How would he respond?"

"He'd say, 'So what makes your opinion of yourself more important than what God has said about your new life in Christ?' He'd make me recite one of the many verses he's had me memorize to remind myself that I'm not who I once was. After that, he would pile on with several more verses until I was so confident of Christ in me that I would do whatever hard thing he had waiting behind them."

"Give me an example of what he might ask you to do."

"You don't know Happy. He doesn't ask. He has this unvarnished way of declaring what's rolling around in my mind but is desperate not to reach the surface."

"What are you resisting saying aloud right now?"

"That I'm scared to meet Lisa and David."

"Fair enough. Why?"

"Because they have grown up into remarkable human beings without me. I'm afraid I would disappointment them."

"You've already done that. Not piling on... just saying. So let's say your worst fears come true. How would that change your relationship with them?"

"Not much, I guess, other than to solidify what they already think about me."

"Understood. Flip it now. What do you stand to gain if you step into this and they forgive you, too?"

"Paula, I'll be honest, I'm hesitant to say. I can't let myself imagine something as unfathomable as a second chance with them. Shoot, I still can't believe you're talking to me right now. I suppose I'm afraid I'll wake up to find this is all a dream."

"So, what would Happy say is your core issue here?"

"Well, if I'm afraid to reach out and scared to imagine this turning out well, it's easy enough to see that my actual issue is fear instead of forgiving myself."

"That wasn't so hard to acknowledge, now, was it?"

"No. And yes."

"Now what would Happy say?"

"He'd ask me when I needed a week's vacation to go to Mississippi."

"And what would you tell him?"

"Soon."

"Would he accept that answer?"

I laughed out loud. "No. He'd pull out his calender and start flipping through it. Then, he'd shoot me a curious glance and say he couldn't find *Soon* on his calendar and tell me to try again. He wouldn't let it go until I had chosen some dates."

"How about you discuss this with Happy and shoot me a text by Monday night to inform me when you'll be here?"

"You should be a counselor. You're good at this."

"Brandon, my favorite part of raising Lisa and David is watching how resilient they are. They bounce back from disappointment better than either of us ever did. Maybe we would have been more like them at their age if we hadn't tried to grow up too fast. They're awesome kids, and they want to know their father. Keep reminding yourself of that."

I hated to end the call, but an hour-and-a-half was long enough. As I clicked the red button to end the call, I pinched myself again to confirm it had been real.

13

"Hey, Happy, I'm calling to apologize for leaving without telling you what was going on tonight."

"We wondered what happened to you. Are you okay?"

"Never better, but I have quite a story to share. Are we still good for tomorrow afternoon?"

"Sure, but don't make me wait until tomorrow. Give me something tonight."

"Happy, you're always pressing me to not sell God short. I don't mean to, but I keep doing it. I was heartbroken when I left the church tonight, thinking Paula was about to push through for a divorce. She had called as I was leaving and wanted me to call her back when I got home. Instead of asking for a divorce, she informed me my children were interested in pursuing a relationship with me. It took me completely by surprise."

"Yet you've been praying for this very thing for months now, haven't you?"

"Every day, several times a day. But I couldn't imagine it actually happening. And now it appears it will."

"I believe..."

"... help my unbelief. I'll fill you in on the details tomorrow. I may need to ask for another chance to address the recovery group because I'm afraid I laced my message tonight with faithlessness."

"We could give you another chance next week to remedy that. We can talk about that tomorrow. Goodnight, Brandon."

"Goodnight, Happy. And thanks."

DURING CHURCH ON SUNDAY, I wiggled and squirmed like a six-year-old boy with too much starch in his collar. I tried to focus on the message, but my mind kept fast forwarding to my afternoon with Happy. I couldn't wait to tell him every detail of my conversation with Paula. Without a doubt, he would uncover a nugget I had missed or offer some insight about next steps or challenge me to pray out of my faith range.

The cool late November Texas air inspired Happy to pull two four-wheelers from the barn, where he was waiting when I pulled up in my Happy Electric truck. "Hop on, and let's ride to the back of my property."

This was a first for me. As many times as I had visited the Hapstead place, I had no idea how much property he owned. To ride to the back of a property in Texas could encompass hours, though I had not imagined Happy's place being more than the few acres I had walked with him. The sign over the main entrance proclaimed "My Happy Place" and included a metalwork smiley face logo similar to the ones on all of Happy's work trucks. The long driveway from the main road to his house invoked visions of a sprawling ranch, but he had never mentioned cattle or timber or repairing fences or the like.

I hopped on the second four-wheeler beside my boss and waited for him to lead the way. After affirming I could operate an off-road vehicle and promising to take it easy since it had been twenty years since I had driven an ATV, he sped away to a gap in the trees. We wound fifteen minutes through the hardwoods until we passed through an opening on the far edge of the woods. Before us lay a lake that stretched for upwards of fifty acres with the curves of multiple inlets to give it shape. A sizable gazebo sat near the end of a peninsula that jutted halfway across the water, threatening to bisect the lake. The trail we traveled led us to it.

"What is this place? This is incredible!"

"This is where I spend my mornings."

"Any fish in there?"

"Oh, sure."

"Big ones?"

"This is Texas, son. What do you think?"

"What's the biggest one you've ever caught?"

"From here—oh, twelve, thirteen pounds."

"Whoa. I used to do a lot of fishing back in Mississippi, but the biggest fish I've ever caught weighed in at barely nine pounds."

"That's a nice one. One day I'll have to bring you back out here to drop a line in the water. Not today, though. You have plenty to tell me today. I hope you didn't eat lunch on the way."

Lunch had slipped my mind. Not Happy's, though. He pulled two steaks from the cooler on the back of his four-wheeler. "These should do just fine." A few minutes later, the steaks sizzled on the gas grill under the gazebo. While we waited, we took in the beauty of the mid-afternoon scene before us.

"You say this is where you spend your mornings?" I asked when Happy stood to flip the steaks. "Fishing and grilling meat?"

Happy shook his head while he tended the steaks. "Reading my Bible and praying for opportunities." When Happy glanced up from the grill, he caught my stare. "Brandon, do you know how I'm always pushing you to believe God is bigger than you imagine Him to be?"

I nodded. "I've been thinking about that a lot over these last few weeks with everything that has happened between Paula and me."

He peered at the lake and swung his arm from left to right. "My number one goal every morning is to be sitting right where you are when the sun comes up over the horizon right there." He pointed to a clearing on the eastern edge of the lake to our right. "When the sun comes up between those two stands of trees, I'm reminded of how small I am in relation to God and His creation. But I also remember that there's nothing beyond His capacity. I find it's when the sun is in that little frame above the horizon and between those trees that I pray my most audacious prayers."

My mind no longer spun with thoughts of the big fish beneath the surface of the placid water before us. This was a holy place, one Happy had never mentioned during all the time he had mentored me. Even as he reached into a cabinet beside the grill to produce plates, forks, and knives, my mind raced to figure out today's occasion. When the steaks were done—but not well done, Happy noted—we sat at a handcrafted picnic table in the center of the gazebo to eat our steak and grilled asparagus. I dared not dive into deeper conversation until I expressed a genuine appreciation for the succulent steak that reminded me I had not eaten since the few bites of supper before my call to Paula.

Happy was swirling a piece of steak in the juices on his plate when he asked me to tell him about my prior night's conversation. I did, breaking social graces by talking and eating simultaneously. The summary of my call with Paula took almost that long to recount to Happy, but he wanted every detail. When I reached the end of our call, he leaned back in his chair and tapped his fingers together to a tune in his head. He reached well back into everything I had told him to mine his nugget.

Instead, Happy returned to his cooler and returned with a sizable container of cold, sliced watermelon. We ate it in silence. It was atypical for Happy to dance around something he wanted to say, but I sensed he was stalling. He stepped from the dock toward a path leading through a stand of woods but motioned me to keep keep my seat. He returned almost an hour later with no explanation, instead nibbling on the last piece of watermelon in the container.

"PAULA SAID SHE HADN'T DATED."

"Huh?"

"She was making another point, but right in the middle of that, she said she hadn't dated since you left."

"I guess she did." I tried again to relate the enormity of my opportunity to reunite with my children. Happy fastened instead that hapless detail of Paula's existence. It didn't line up with the man who woke early each morning to meet with God in this place.

Happy walked to the edge of the gazebo that hung out over the water and stared at the horizon. After several minutes, he turned back toward where I was still sitting. "Brandon, I'm not one to announce that God has told me something very often. I hear from Him every day, but I choose to let Him speak for Himself most of the time. But I'm going to share something with you that I believe He impressed on me."

This was a depth of Happy's walk with God that I had never seen. It seemed a place in their relationship that he couldn't tell me, but had to show me. He pointed again to the opening on the eastern shore.

"There. Everyone who applies for a job at Happy Electric goes through a vetting process that includes at least fifteen minutes of a sunrise in that opening. I ask the Lord to show me anything He wants me to see that goes beyond words on an application or a resumé. I might be dead set to hire someone, but the Lord has shown me here what a disaster that hire could be. Sometimes my opinion is that a potential employee won't fit with us, but God directs me otherwise, and I hire him. Or her."

"Which category did I fit into before you hired me?"

Happy continued, as if he hadn't heard me. "I trust Him more that I trust my own decisions. When my idea of an employee conflicts with His, I go with God. Brandon, I almost hired some people who would have undone much of the culture we've built at Happy Electric. Likewise, I almost missed out on some incredible employees. God would have continued to work in their lives somewhere else, but I prefer to be up close and personal to the God stories happening every day in our Happy Electric family."

Happy turned back toward me for just a second, as if reminding himself who stood in his special spot with him. "When I brought your name to the Lord the morning after I met you, he revealed He would show me wonderful and mighty works through you such as I had never seen. He also impressed upon me that I would need to encourage and challenge you along the way. I asked for specifics on what He wanted to accomplish through you."

"What did He say?"

Happy continued staring out over the western end of the lake, where the sun was dipping toward the tops of the trees. Here, too, I noticed a gap in the trees surrounding the water. During his prolonged silence, I observed the battle continuing in Happy's soul. He brought me to his most intimate place to share something with me, but the words didn't flow.

"Brandon, I've spent many a morning watching the sun rise above this lake and calling out to the Lord on your behalf. You're unlike anyone I've ever discipled since you don't fall into the usual patterns. The Lord has had to guide me more than with anyone else. while I was sitting right there where you're sitting, He told me to slot you with Jacob and C.J. He told me to draw you into the recovery group even though you weren't an addict, at least not in the clinical sense. After you shared your past with me..." He trailed off, watching the sun creep toward the horizon.

"What else, Happy? God showed you something else about me, didn't He?"

"Brandon, it's not very often I bring one of my employees out here, even one I'm discipling. I wanted you to see something I hope you'll never forget." He twirled around and stepped to the cooler to fetch a bottle of water. "Need another one?"

"Sure."

He tossed me a plastic bottle and twisted the cap on his own. After taking a lengthy gulp, he pulled the bottle from his lips. "Ahh. Come here and check out one of the most incredible sights I have ever seen." He beckoned me to join him in a pair of chairs sitting on the dock that extended from the gazebo. Once seated, he extended his bottle of water toward the lake. The sun had settled into the space between the trees, where its rays bounced off the surface of the water in the gorgeous purple and pink hues of the afternoon sky.

"The Lord gives me direction on that end of the lake in the mornings," Happy said, jerking his thumb over his shoulder. "In the evenings on days like today, He and I sit and talk about what He has done. Brandon, I don't invite many people—even my wife—to join me here, except on rare occasions. I wanted you to see this, though, and celebrate here today with me who God is and what He's done."

"Thank you, Happy," I answered in a whisper. For the next fifteen minutes, we worshiped without a sound as the sun gradually sank below the horizon with only the sounds of nature. I have never felt closer to God.

"There's more that God revealed to you about me, isn't there, Happy?" I asked at last.

He squared his shoulders toward me, took a deep breath, and released it. "We'd better be getting back while we still have light." He strapped the cooler to his four-wheeler and led the way back through the woods without another word. When we had parked them in the barn, he thanked me for coming and told me he would see me at work the next morning.

"Happy, please…"

Halfway to his front porch, he turned slowly. "She said 'I didn't date.'" He continued to the front door without another word.

"Wait, what? Happy…" The click of the front door bid me goodnight.

14

At three o'clock in the morning, still staring at the ceiling, I typed out a text I intended to send to Paula before I drove to work on Monday morning. I had counted nine times I had rolled over and tried to sleep. I might as well accomplish something during my sleepless night.

•Hey, Paula, I haven't been able to stop thinking about our talk Saturday night. I spent the afternoon with Happy yesterday. I didn't get around to asking him for vacation time, but I wanted to ask you if it would be okay if I drove to Harriston at the end of the week. I'm sure he could make it a few days without me. What do you think about meeting me Thursday and maybe setting up something with the kids on Friday or Saturday?

I SET my phone on my nightstand and rolled over to try for the tenth time to doze off for the rest of the night. About the time I had settled into a comfortable position on my side, I heard my phone buzz. A text from Paula. *Oh, crap, I hit send.*

> That sounds good. Send me some details after you talk to your boss. I won't say anything to Lisa or David until you finish planning your trip. What's keeping you up so late at night?

NICE GOING, sport.

> So sorry, I couldn't sleep, so I typed out this text but didn't plan to send it until before work. Sorry to wake you.

I SENT THE TEXT, not expecting another response. I rolled over for attempt number eleven to grab a few hours' sleep before I needed to get up for work.

> It's okay. I woke up an hour ago and couldn't go back to sleep. Why can't you sleep?

THREE-THIRTY. THREE HOURS' sleep, tops.

> Happy took me to a special spot at the back of his place yesterday. I told him about what you told me Saturday night, and he shared some stuff with me that has had my mind racing ever since.

I SENT the text and rolled over for attempt number twelve at sleep. As soon as I settled in, I glanced back over my shoulder. Nothing. Two deep breaths. And then my phone buzzed.

> Wanna talk?

YES, yes, a thousand times yes.

> Sure.

WAIT, is she going to call me? Should I call her? Of course I should. Dial the number, stupid, while you can still do it first. Don't call me stupid—you don't dial numbers on a cell phone. Who you calling stupid?

Paula's sleepy voice answering my call hushed the competing voices. "Couldn't sleep, huh?"

"Two nights in a row now. I can't believe how God is answering my prayers to give me the opportunity to say *I'm sorry* to you and Lisa and David. I trusted Him, and I begged Him, but I'm still surprised He answered."

"A lot of water under the bridge. And over it. I'm just now seeing the bridge again."

"Same here. I keep hoping the bridge is still sound. I'm afraid it will break."

"Brandon, have you paid attention to how many times you have mentioned that you're afraid of this or scared of that?"

"Yes, and I hate it. Tell me, Paula, is this real?"

"Brandon, it's four o'clock in the morning and we're talking on the phone to each other after twenty years of nothing. It's time to test whether the bridge will hold. Don't let fear keep you from coming to Mississippi to see your children."

"There's no danger of that. It's just…"

"Quit adding the doubt at the end. Let it be what it's going to be and deal with what's real."

"*Deal with what's real*. You should print that on a T-shirt. I'd buy one. So… what are Lisa and David saying about my trip to see them?"

"Don't over analyze. Just show up."

"O-kay."

"Sorry, I didn't mean to be rude, but you'll be fine. You're coming Thursday?"

"If that's okay with you. I don't think Happy will have a problem with it. I haven't missed a day of work since I started."

Paula waited before saying, "You really have turned over a new leaf." Her delivery came across as more statement than question.

"I didn't turn it over. Jesus did. I wanted to—don't get me wrong—but I couldn't do it on my own. Now, I have the power to follow through with my best intentions, to take the first step toward something that I wouldn't have before I gave my life to Him. It helps to have Happy and Jacob in my ear every day, pushing me in the direction I need to go. Sometimes, I can't tell the difference between God's voice and Happy's."

"What did he say today that's got you talking to your long-estranged wife at 4:23 on a Monday morning before we both have to go to work?"

"Give me a minute to think through the answer to that question. The entire afternoon was so… unexpected." I paused until the silence grew awkward, at least on my end. "To visit Happy's most intimate place in the world… wow. I've been to his house dozens of times, but he had never even told me about his lake. The four-wheeler ride was fun—it had been a while since I had ridden one. And then, the lake—it was stunning. You remember how much I used to love to fish."

"Oh, yeah." *Ouch. Not the best angle to arrive at what I don't want to tell her.*

"Well, I haven't gone fishing since I moved here. My gear is still in the back of the hall closet, where it has been since I moved in twenty years ago. Man, twenty years in this dump. I need to find a new place. Do you and Lisa and David still live in that same house?"

"No, we moved into an apartment closer to campus when Lisa started school so she could walk to school most days. David bought his own truck as soon as he got his driver's license, but we couldn't afford a vehicle for Lisa, so this made the most sense. She borrows my car or David's truck or rides with Jake anywhere she needs to go. It's an inconvenience sometimes, but she has never complained. She understands how incredible her opportunity to attend college for free is."

"Where does David keep his lawn equipment?"

"He has a storage unit a block over from our apartment. We call it his other house."

"Nice. It's awesome how he's built up his business, even while he was serving overseas."

"It is. But you've gotten way off track."

Nice try, Gull. Or Wade. "I was saying that Happy's lake captivated my attention. We pulled into a peninsula that juts out over the middle of it. He has this sweet setup at the end of it—a pavilion with a deck right out over the water. He unstrapped a cooler from the back of his four-wheeler and pulled out two steaks and threw them on a grill he keeps down there. The former me would have carried a fishing rod in one hand and a cold beer in the other straight down to the lake. Yesterday, though, I soaked in the glory of what I guess you could call Happy's happy place. I didn't realize I hadn't eaten since before you called last night, but that steak was amazing."

"You're getting off track again."

She won't settle for anything less than everything. "Happy showed me this gap in the trees that surround the lake. It's where he goes most mornings to watch the sunrise and to pray for people like me. He said the Lord gives him direction about who to hire and who not to and how to disciple the ones he hires. Later, he showed me a gap on the other side where he watches the sun set when he wants to thank the Lord for answers to the prayers he's prayed in the other direction."

"Sounds like a special place."

"Unlike anywhere I've ever been. You think you know somebody, and then they say something that makes you wonder if you ever knew them at all."

"Yep." The word was definitive with a pop to the *p* and aimed at me, I hoped.

"I've told you before how Happy pushed me to pray for an opportunity to beg you and Lisa and David for your forgiveness. When you showed up here... well, let's just say I wish I had a better place than my apartment to say thank You to the Lord. Happy says the lake and the sunrises and sunsets keep him humble and make him realize his smallness compared to God. Paula, you were so gracious that I'm still overwhelmed. So much more than I deserved."

"It wouldn't be forgiveness or mercy if I gave you what you deserved. Trust me, it took every bit of twenty years to bring me to that point. You, too, to listen to your story."

"It shouldn't have taken so long. For me, anyway. One of my God-sized questions He hasn't answered yet is why it had to take so long. Paula, I was so close several times to walking away from my punkheaded lifestyle, but every time, something out of the ordinalry dragged me back into it. Why wouldn't He want to call me before I did so much damage to you and the kids and myself? I don't get it."

"Neither do I. Pastor Hobbs had to walk me through

that. When he talks about understanding God's ways, you listen. He almost lost his brother to a freak drug overdose. He lost everything in Hurricane Katrina and moved to this area and built an amazing life with his wife. They impacted more folks in their time in Harriston than most do in a lifetime, but then one of the very people she was trying to help murdered her. It all seems so random, but he somehow loves the Lord more now than ever. I don't know if you have ever studied the book of Job in the Bible…"

"Twice. Once in church and once with Jacob."

"Well, Pastor Hobbs is a modern-day Job. He says that we should visit the past when we have something there that needs fixing and we're still able to fix it, but that we must live in the present."

"Deal with the real."

"That's what he tells me every time we talk and I try to wallow in regret. You didn't think I made that up, did you?"

"Doesn't matter. I need to remember it."

As the time moved toward 5:30, we reached the awkward part of the conversation where neither of us had anything ready to say. Either of us might have claimed it time to arise and prepare for work. Both of us would struggle to make it through a Monday following an eventful weekend and a sleepless Sunday night. Paula interrupted the interlude by asking if Happy had said anything after we watched the sunset. Caught between painful honesty and the wisdom of waiting to reveal my desire to be reunited to my wife, I groaned. She heard it.

"He told you, didn't he?"

"Told me what?"

"Are you going to force me to say it?" Her voice possessed an edge not present before.

"Paula, I…"

"I called Happy. There, I said it. Happy?"

"Uh… what about him?"

"No, are you happy?"

"Gotcha," I snickered. "I thought you meant…"

She didn't find the word play funny. "Brandon, what happened to being honest with one another?"

"Paula, listen to me. This is the first I've heard of a conversation between you and Happy. Honest."

"I had to know. I'm sorry."

"Had to know what? Sorry for what? You're leaving out a considerable chunk."

Paula sniffed, sighed, and started from the beginning. "I didn't have any plans for anything but an apology when I drove to Texas. I expected you to be the same old Brandon, which your apartment complex confirmed, or so I thought. But then you walked out to your truck to drive to dinner, looking like a normal human being. When you talked about how the Lord was working in your life, He heaped conviction on me for selling Him short. I guess the victim in me gave me the sense I was superior to you somehow. On the drive home, I released some more bitterness and thanked the Lord for changing your life, like He had changed mine. It still didn't seem fair that He saved you first, but I made the first move toward reconciliation. Is that the right word? I'm still learning from Pastor Hobbs."

"Yeah, that's it. Tell me something, Paula. Is this all real?"

"I wish you would quit asking that, but I'll be honest, I ask myself the same question every day. Yet we're talking on the phone at almost 6:00 in the morning. I start a new job the Monday after Lisa's wedding, so I'm thinking today might be a sick day."

"Where's your new job?"

"I'll be working for Stapleford Construction here in Harriston. Vicki Stapleford and her sons own it. I told you earlier that she is Pastor Hobbs's fiancee."

"You swinging a hammer?"

"Not on your life. Working in their office, helping coordinate the work that the various crews do and making sure they have what they need at their job sites."

"Emily."

"Huh?"

"Sorry, the job you described is what Emily Huff does at Happy Electric. She takes the calls from our guys in the field and sends me to them with whatever they need. You'll discover how forgetful guys in the construction field can be."

"I'm sure."

"So you talked to Happy about me?"

"You asked me a few minutes ago if this was real. That question lingered for days after I returned to my routine here, but—don't hate me for this—I couldn't trust what my eyes were seeing and my ears were hearing. The past reared up in my mind and warned me not to fall for…"

"It's okay. So you did a background check, of sorts."

"I'm sorry."

"Paula, I wouldn't expect you to take me at my word. For crying out loud, you found me from my police record. To tell you the truth, it stunned me when you said yes to grabbing a bite to eat. I'll also confess that I didn't shower beforehand. I dropped to my knees and begged God to keep me from blowing the opportunity you had given me. The entire time we were eating and talking, I was afraid you would bolt."

"For the record, I couldn't tell you hadn't showered, but it was apparent how nervous you were. It's one reason I stayed, not because I enjoyed it, but it gave your story more validity."

"Not enough, though."

"I called Happy last Saturday, the week before Thanksgiving. He might want to rethink putting his personal cell phone number on his company website after a call from a random female stranger."

"You're no stranger to Happy, I can assure you. He has called out your name to the Lord at sunrise along with mine. He told me as much."

"Funny, now that you mention it, he didn't seem surprised by my call, and he assured me he wasn't doing anything important that morning. Anyway, I told him who I was and why I was calling. He couldn't say enough about the work the Lord had done in your life and how consistent you were at 'showing up,' he called it. Even though he sang your praises, I came away with the feeling that Happy is a straight shooter and wasn't taking sides, if that makes sense."

"For sure. Since I shared my story with him, he has taken your side, which is understandable."

"We didn't talk super long, but he convinced me he was a fine judge of character. Now that I know about how he prays over people at sunrise at his lake, I understand why. Anyway, I shouldn't be saying this to you, but, for better or worse, I have decided to trust you, Brandon."

For better or worse? A turn of a phrase? What else did Happy say to Paula?

"Paula, I need to leave for work at seven, and I barely have time for a shower. I'm so sorry, but I need to go."

"Oh, you'll take a shower for work, but not for me?"

"Guilty."

"Okay, I'll let you go."

"Have a good day."

"You, too. Bye." The line went dead.

"Paula, Happy said something else…"

15

"Paula?"

No answer. In a roundabout way, the end of our two-and-half-hour phone conversation led to where I sensed it would. Even though I added the last piece of the puzzle that we had both tried to assemble after she ended the call, I had said it out loud. Perhaps I could say it again to Paula over dinner Thursday night. On the drive to work, I rehearsed asking Happy for two days off this week and two more in three weeks when my baby girl would marry this Jake guy. My baby girl, whom I hadn't seen since she was in diapers.

I couldn't shake my nerves when I stepped into Happy's office and asked for a minute of his time. So many times in the last decade, I stepped near the edge of radical changes to my life, only to retreat into the known, as pitiful as it might have been. The *what ifs* had threatened to overwhelm me on my commute. A sleepless night didn't help keep them at bay, though adrenaline propelled me into Happy's office before fear reeled in my best intentions. The most effective weapon I have found against my fear is voicing my intentions, especially to Happy.

"HAPPY, I didn't sleep a wink last night."

"What's wrong? Did the steak sit wrong on your stomach?"

"No, the steak was delicious. Thanks again for that and for sharing your special place with me yesterday."

"What's the matter?"

"Nothing's wrong. I couldn't get your words out of my mind."

"Which ones?"

"She didn't date."

Happy smiled, propping his elbows on the arms of his chair and tapping his fingers against one another. "Go on."

"I played out one scenario after another in my mind. Does God want to restore our marriage? In the deepest part of my mind, I hope for that, but the realist in me won't allow my thoughts to run in that direction for long."

"Let me stop you right there, Brandon. Is it the realist in you or is it your fear that doesn't let you imagine what you and I both know is what God wants. Your twenty-year hiatus is not His roadmap to a godly marriage—I'll acknowledge that—but what are the chances a couple splits up, never follows through with a divorce, and refrains from dating for two decades? I would say zero or right next to it. And yet…"

"This is where you've been leading me since I told you my story. How did you know?"

"I didn't, but God did. I remember the first time I prayed your name toward the eastern gap in the trees. God told me He was going to do a work in your life that I had not seen in anyone else I had ever mentored. I have a hard time not running ahead of Him in this, but I believe He gave me permission yesterday on the ride back from the lake."

"Well, when I still hadn't fallen asleep at three o'clock this morning, I typed out a text to Paula asking if I could come to Mississippi this coming weekend. I figured if I could visualize the words, I could grab a few hours' sleep and send the text at a decent hour. I laid my phone on the table next to my bed and rolled over. Evidently, I hit send on accident because my phone buzzed right after that with a text from Paula. Long story short, we texted back and forth for a few minutes and ended up talking on the phone until six-thirty."

"Good?"

"Yes, very good. If Happy Electric can survive without me Thursday and Friday, I'd like to go to Mississippi to meet my children. Be warned, though: if this goes well, I'll be asking for another day or two around December fifteenth for Lisa's wedding. I'm trying not to be overly optimistic, but things seem to be trending in that direction."

"If you don't blow it this weekend." It was a rare caustic remark from Happy. I felt my head tilt to the right and my brow furrow. He let his words sit for a moment and continued, "That's what running through your mind, isn't it?"

"I'm fighting it, but, yeah."

"Why did it bother you when I said it?"

"Because you're the force behind the smiley faces on all the trucks out there," I said, waving my hand toward his door that opened into the warehouse. "You're Mr. Optimistic. You're... you're... Happy."

"Why do you think that is?"

"You're a gift from God to so many of us here, Happy. I suppose He blessed you with such a positive outlook so you would have what it took to reach us knuckleheads."

"That's true to a degree, I suppose, but my story includes plenty of heartache, too. And, true, being such an optimist brings its share of disappointment, but one day all the hard parts of this life will become untrue. One glorious day, Jesus will return to earth, and He will make all things right. Every once in a while, though, God gives us a glimpse of the restorative work He continues to do through redeeming a hopeless situation. Brandon, I believe with every ounce of my being that God is going to restore you and Paula and restore the years that the locusts have eaten away."

"Locusts?"

"Figurative language from the book of Joel in the Old Testament."

"Gotcha."

"Look, Brandon, I can't guarantee beyond any doubt that I'm hearing from God about you and Paula. I'm pretty sure I am, but I've been wrong before, and I'll be wrong again. But what do you lose by following where God appears to be leading? I mean, if this doesn't pan out with Paula and your children, will you be more estranged from them then than now?

"I guess not. You sound like Paula."

"Take Thursday and Friday then, and go to Mississippi with the mindset that God will continue what He has started. Enjoy the journey. When can we expect you back?"

"Monday."

"Okay. Stay longer if you need." Happy stood to indicate I could check with Emily for my first assignment of the day.

"Thanks, Happy."

"You're welcome."

"Oh, and, Happy?"

"Yes?"

"You didn't tell me Paula called you."

"You never asked."

I grinned, "No, I suppose I didn't."

BETWEEN SLEEP DEPRIVATION and anticipation of the long weekend, the rest of the day was a blur. After my last delivery, I stopped to fill my work truck with gas before heading home. I was closer to my apartment than the shop, so a mere fifteen minutes stood between me and the nap I had been craving all afternoon. I would sleep for an hour, eat, text Paula to confirm my plans, and go to bed before nine o'clock. When I curled the gas receipt inside the cup holder to save for Tuesday morning, I saw a text notification from Happy.

Drop by the shop before you head home today.

I groaned and turned into the traffic I would have avoided. Twenty minutes later, I plopped into the seat opposite Happy's desk. He asked what was the matter.

"I was fifteen minutes from a nap to start catching up from a sleepless night." I told him where I had been when I received his text.

"Sorry, this could have waited until tomorrow morning. I checked the schedule and saw you were near the Aspen site."

"Carlos needed a can light for the Cartwright job, and I had one in my truck, so Emily asked me to run it by before quitting time. She probably didn't write it on the board."

"No, and she left early for her daughter's soccer game."

"It's okay."

"I won't keep you long, but I wanted to give you something." Happy reached into his desk drawer and tossed a key in my direction. Its smiley face key chain said it would fit a company truck.

"Figured you could break in your new truck on the drive to Mississippi."

"But I thought..."

"I decided not to wait a year. Plus, I'm not sure the truck you've been driving is interstate worthy. We'll get it serviced and use it as an extra around the shop, maybe pass it along to the next new hire looking to see how God can change his life."

"Thanks, Happy. I had planned to rent a car, but…"

"You can still do that if you'd rather not show up in a company truck."

"I don't mind."

"Good. Use the money you would have spent to take your wife to a fancy restaurant and court her right."

My stomach flipped, not at the idea of spending money on taking Paula to a nice place but at considering it a date. No matter how she had engaged in conversation with me in the middle of the previous night, it seemed forward. I'm not sure what would have convinced me to call it anything other than a meeting with my children's mother to prepare to re-engage with them.

"Happy, you buy a lot of vehicles, don't you?"

"More than the average Joe."

"I'm considering buying a car."

The tilt of his head questioned why. "Brandon, you can drive the company truck like it's your own. Wouldn't you rather put a down payment on a house before you buy something that will depreciate like a car?"

"Please don't think me ungrateful, Happy, but I believe it's something I need to do."

"Fine. I'll get my guy to hook you up with a deal. Promise you won't buy a brand new car, though. You'll pay at least two thousand to drive if off the lot."

"Deal. How about a late model sedan that still smells new? Will you approve one like that?"

"I'll give my guy a call after you walk out that door. Now, stay awake at the wheel and drive your new truck home."

At the same time I walked through my front door, my phone buzzed. I reached for it immediately, hoping it was Paula calling. Instead, it was an unknown local number. I let it go to voice mail, which I checked before lying down for a few minutes before supper.

"Hey, Brandon, this is Woody Jeffries down at Richardson Motors. Kerry Hapstead told me to call you when I come across a good deal on a late model sedan. I got one in yesterday that the service department checked off this afternoon—great car, thirty miles to the gallon, three years old, low mileage. If we put it on the lot, it'll be gone by the end of the day tomorrow. If you can get here by seven tonight, I can let you have it for five hundred over my cost as a friend of Happy's." I groaned again and grabbed my new key.

16

Tuesday and Wednesday passed in a blink. Happy called me to his office both mornings and both afternoons to make sure my new truck was driving well and getting good gas mileage. I recognized his true purpose and kidded him by rising to leave after I answered his initial question each time. I settled back in to update him on my conversations with Paula, which grew shorter as we attempted to recover from a sleepless Sunday night. On Wednesday afternoon Happy wished me a productive trip and sent me home an hour early to pack. Even after I told him my bag was packed and sitting by the front door, he waved me off and instructed me to enjoy an extra hour's sleep.

At five o'clock on Thursday morning, armed with a duffel bag, three sets of hanging clothes, and a thermos of black coffee, I set out for Harriston, Mississippi. A Grisham audiobook accompanied me on the seven-and-a-half hour drive across I-20, but it soon became background noise. Scenario after scenario played out in my mind. Paula had cajoled me to leave my fears in Texas, that Mississippi didn't have room for them. Happy had encouraged me to not limit what God wanted to do to restore my marriage. I couldn't help searching for potential snags, though I fought to keep negative thoughts at bay.

With only two bathroom breaks and a quick drive-through breakfast outside of Shreveport, I stayed on schedule. A little before one o'clock, I needed a break, so I stopped west of Jackson, Mississippi, in a little town called Clinton to eat lunch at a chicken restaurant. As I turned into town from the interstate, I glanced down the hill from Highway 80 to the stately campus of Mississippi College. College students dotted the landscape below, rushing to their next classes and strolling on the lawn in no particular hurry. I wondered how my life might have been different if I had taken advantage of my opportunity to earn a college degree.

In my mind's eye, I swatted away the what if's as I walked into the restaurant, which was more off the beaten path than I realized but still packed. I replaced the regrets with visions of Paula and me walking together into a similar restaurant in Harriston soon. After I placed my order for a chicken sandwich meal—which gave the chipper college girl behind the counter great pleasure—I stepped to the corner of the counter to wait. An older lady stood there, refilling cups at customers' requests. Hers, too, was a pleasurable job, to hear her tell it.

"What makes you so happy today?"

It took a moment for me to realize she was addressing me. "Me? Oh, nothing."

"You sure have a big smile on your face."

"I didn't realize it. Truth is, I'm on my way to reconcile with my wife and children after twenty years."

"Would it be too forward if I offered to pray for you?" she asked.

"Ms. Doris," I said, reading her name tag, "that would be tremendous."

"Dear Lord," she started, not hesitating for a moment except to put her hand on my shoulder and pray for me, "I lift—honey, I clean forgot to ask your name."

"Brandon."

"Lord, I lift Brandon to you and ask that you strengthen him to say *I'm sorry* with all of his might and to mean it. I pray You would cause his wife and kids to believe him all the way to the level he means his apology. And may you get the glory, Lord, for what you're going to do through this man and his family. In the powerful name of Jesus I pray, amen."

"Thank you, Ms. Doris."

"Honey, you're welcome. Sara, you can give this man his food now."

The girl at the counter—Sara, as it were—handed me a tray with a smile. I thanked her, though she insisted the pleasure was all hers. Ten minutes later, I hugged Ms. Doris and hopped back in my truck, literally and figuratively full and eager to face the two remaining hours on the road.

AT THREE O'CLOCK on the dot, I wheeled into the parking lot of Paula's apartment complex and walked straight toward her building. A balding gentleman stood in front of Apartment 4A and eyed me as I ascended the stairs to 3B. I knocked on the door and waited. When no answered within a few seconds, I raised my hand to knock again at the same time Paula opened the door.

"Whoa," she said, ducking. "Trying to land the first punch?"

"No, I..."

"I'm kidding." She stepped onto the threshold and wrapped her right arm around my waist. I slipped my left arm around her shoulder, squeezed, and released as soon as she did. "I'm glad you made it okay. Any problems on the road?"

"No, easy as could be expected. The truckers rode side by side sometimes, but overall, not too bad. A lady at the restaurant in Clinton where I stopped for lunch even prayed for me. Do I appear that nervous?"

"I don't believe so. Are you?"

"Not too bad. Your security guard didn't stop me."

"Security guard?"

"Posted in front of 4A."

"Oh, Rodney. Lisa and David like to joke that he has a thing for me because he helps carry my groceries upstairs sometimes. I take the high road and suggest he's being a gentleman, but I try not to encourage him past common courtesy."

"Probably a good idea. You look great." Paula wore comfortable jeans and casual boots with a lightweight burnt orange sweater that highlighted her deep brown eyes and her dark brown hair that appeared to have had a recent color. It was her smile, though, that reminded me why she drew my attention the first time I laid eyes on her.

"Thanks. You look like you could use a shower. Have you checked into your hotel yet?"

"No, I thought I'd stop here first and check in with you. Sorry if I smell. I promise to clean up before we go eat this time."

She laughed. I joined her. Then, an awkward silence accentuated the gap between the small talk of the moment and the deep words to be spoken over the following three days. I asked about Lisa and David. Lisa and Jake would be shopping for items for their new house until the stores closed. David planned to clean and service his equipment until his mother texted him to return home.

"Have you chosen a restaurant?" I asked.

"You said *nice*. Are you talking sit down nice or fancy nice?"

"Khakis and a button-down nice."

Paula smiled. "I have a new dress I've been wanting to wear. Lisa bought it for me, but I haven't had an opportunity to wear it."

"Cool. Is 5:30 too early?"

"No, that's fine. It might take me that long to put myself together."

I wanted to say she looked put together enough already, but I resisted. "What color is your dress?"

"It's kind of medium brown."

"Will a royal blue striped shirt match okay?"

"Sure, I think so."

"Okay, I'll go check in and get ready." I was standing on the landing outside, and the door was almost closed behind me. "Paula?"

"Yeah?" A hint of her smile remained.

"Is this a date?"

"We'll see," she answered with a coy smile before closing the door. I was still grinning when I passed Rodney in front of 4A and nodded.

I RETURNED to Paula's apartment two hours later, clean and shaven and nervous as a cat in a room full of rocking chairs. Rodney gave me a once-over as I passed his watch in front of 4A, his approval assumed in his silence. When I lifted my hand to rap on Paula's door, I attempted in vain to keep my fist from shaking. She answered my knock quicker this time, and my knees buckled when she did.

Dressed in a modest knee-length brown sweater dress with matching suede knee boots, she struck me as stunning. She wore a royal blue scarf with brown and white accents that propelled her outfit from dressy casual to classy. I felt outdressed and outclassed. Doubts and insecurities rushed to fill the gap I sensed between us. If she hadn't spoken, the voices may have told me to run.

"Hey."

"Hey, yourself. Wow, am I underdressed? I didn't bring a jacket—not that I keep many dinner jackets." It struck me that perhaps Paula felt a need to outdress me in order to keep control of our conversation. Any attempt to hush the voices in my head proved futile, so I prayed hard that God would allow me to see and trust what was real.

"You're fine. Let me grab my purse and we'll go."

"Which restaurant did you pick?"

"Steak place out west of town. You won't believe how much that area has grown. So you know, I don't do fancy restaurants. Jake and Lisa ate there on one of their dating anniversaries and couldn't say enough about how delicious the food was. I didn't even ask if that was okay."

"I'm good with whatever."

"Earlier this afternoon, you asked if this was a date."

I felt my face flush and realized that my telltale red neck would give away my embarrassment at having been so forward. "Yeah, sorry, that was out of line."

"Are you paying?"

"Yes, of course," I said, delighted by a concrete question with a straightforward answer.

"Then let's consider it like a first date, one where we're on our best behavior."

"Where it's okay to be nervous?"

"That would be tremendous."

"If I stumble all over myself, that's expected?"

"And reciprocated."

"That's a date I can handle." I offered my arm, which she took. As we walked toward the stairs, I added, "I'll be honest with you, I'm not real up on the dating scene. It has been a while."

"Same."

"You'll turn every head at the restaurant."

Paula stopped on the landing and looked me in the eye. "That was awkward."

"Needed to be said."

She smiled and brushed away hair that wasn't out of place. "Not as awkward as a couple on their first date discussing their children."

"I can't wait."

"Me either. Hey, Rodney."

Paula's security guard's jaw dropped when we passed without looking back. "H-hey, Paula. You going on a date?"

Glancing over her left shoulder as we continued toward my truck, she answered, "Yeah, with my husband. This is Brandon." We left Rodney standing dumbfounded in front of 4A, chuckling as we drove away. Hers seemed to be a giddy, self-confident giggle. Mine was nervous energy, searching for an outlet.

THE HARRISTON I left ended at the hospital on the west side of town. Now, as we topped the hill in that direction, restaurants, strip malls, and office buildings filled the space as far as the eye could see. I pointed to the mall on the right side of the four-lane road as we sat in bumper-to-bumper traffic.

"They built it at last, huh?" Rumors of a mall on that end of town had circulated since the eighties, but its reality surprised me.

"Yeah, a while back. I've only been twice, once when it first opened and once with Lisa to take her Christmas shopping."

"To look at you, I'd think you shopped there for the latest fashions. I can't get over how classy you look."

"Like I told you earlier, Lisa bought me the dress, which I've never worn before tonight. The boots are Lisa's, too. She and I wear the same size in everything, but she doesn't borrow many of my clothes. She's a smart dresser, though, so she had her boots in mind when she bought the dress."

"What about the scarf? It makes the outfit."

"That, I picked out all by myself." Paula arched her shoulders, proud that her purchase caught my attention more than Lisa's choices.

"Boutique shopping, no doubt."

"Goodwill. It's where I buy most of my clothes. Old habits die hard."

"Bought my only suit at the Goodwill in Richardson."

"For church?"

"For court. I wore it to church once, and Happy informed me I overdressed, so I haven't worn it since." I sneaked another glance at Paula. "Traffic always this bad?"

"Afraid so. It's not too much farther, maybe half a

mile ahead on the left. You'll want to move over to the left lane at your earliest opportunity."

Fifteen minutes later, we pulled into the parking lot of the Magnolia Steakhouse, a swankier place than either of us had ever been. As we eased through the crowded parking lot, I noted Lexus, Mercedes, BMW, Range Rover, Cadillac, Porsche, Hummer. My Happy Electric Chevrolet work truck seemed drawn toward the back entrance, as if I was here to change out a light fixture. *What are you thinking, Brandon? The city has passed you by and so has Paula. You're out of your league.*

"Hey, if you want to eat somewhere a little less fancy, I'm okay with that." Is she saying that to bail me out or does she feel exposed, too?

"You know what, Paula? We have as much right to a gourmet meal at a fancy restaurant as these rich people, even if we can't afford it often. We'll park here in the back and stroll to the front like we arrived in the Corvette right there. You'll have every woman in there shopping for your Goodwill scarf at all the finest boutiques in town tomorrow. Come on. Wait..." I walked around the truck to open her door and offered my arm again. "Shall we?" *Lord, has she never been treated like this?* If you restore my marriage, I'll do everything I can to make sure she never feels neglected again.

"Can we imagine we came in that one?" Paula asked, pointing on the sly toward a jet black Audi.

"Sure, that'll work. Shall we name her?"

"Marguerite."

"Excuse me?"

"Her name—Marguerite. It's a character in a book I read. That car makes a perfect Marguerite."

"If you say so."

"I say so." With that, Paula's countenance and gait exuded confidence as we strode toward the door.

Twenty minutes later, the hostess led us to a candlelit table on the left side of the dining room. The plentiful space between tables was perfect for private conversation. She wasted no time.

"Okay, here's what I have lined up for tomorrow. You'll come over for breakfast in the morning around nine, not too early. Lisa doesn't have class on Fridays, and David's guys can handle their work without him for a day. After we eat, I'll have an errand to run that will take about two hours. If you're still in town when I return, we'll take a drive around town to show you what you've missed over the last twenty years. Jake will meet us for lunch after his eleven o'clock class and cast his vote. If nobody blackballs you, we'll eat dinner at our apartment tomorrow night and send you back to your hotel with a thumbs up or thumbs down for the rest of the weekend. After you leave, we'll talk about you and how much we want you to be a part of each of our lives."

"Sounds like y'all have stacked the deck against me."

The pleasant smile on Paula's face disappeared. "Brandon, I believe the Lord has done an amazing work in your life. But if Lisa, David, or even Jake have reservations, I will trust their instincts more than I do my own. I'm not trying to be Debbie Downer here, but you need to understand the gravity of this weekend. If you're not all in, I'm praying somebody senses it."

With every ounce of sincerity I could muster, I nodded and left it at that.

"I shouldn't tell you this," Paula added, "but I'm pulling for you."

17

My enthusiasm for my date with Paula took a hit with her blunt summary of the weekend's schedule. I was committed to earning my family's favor and trust, though, and Paula was behind me, so I fought my way through my temporary doldrums. I remembered Ms. Doris at the restaurant in Clinton had prayed that when my enthusiasm waned, the Lord would fill me with His Spirit. Right on time, Paula asked, "What has God taught you this week?"

"I was drawn like a magnet to the Psalms this week. God showed me in Psalm 77 that He made a way for the Israelites through the Red Sea that nobody but God recognized was there. Goodness, Paula, I still can't believe I'm sitting in Harriston, Mississippi, eating steak above my pay grade with a date who's definitely out of my league."

"I never actually said this was a date," she said, tucking her chin to hide her sheepish smile.

"You didn't say it wasn't."

"Touché."

"Either way, it's the closest thing I've had to a date in over twenty years. Can you imagine that, a good-looking guy like me?"

"You clean up well enough. You seriously haven't been on a single date since you left Harriston?"

"Not one. It's like I stepped into a bubble as far as that goes."

"Brandon, I haven't dated either."

"You're kidding. Not at all? I mean, look at you."

"I'm married. It was a convenient excuse for the creeps who showed some interest. Most of the time, though, I involved myself so much in the kids' lives that I didn't consider a social life beyond theirs. I didn't make many friends, either, until I met my Lonesome, party of six crew. Since I started going to Pastor Hobbs's church, I have gone to some family night suppers and such. I would probably be more comfortable going to church somewhere else—like the church Lisa and Jake attend sometimes—but Pastor Hobbs led me to the Lord. He and his new wife have invited me to join them for supper when they come to town several times. I feel like a third wheel, but I've gone with them since they encourage and invest in me."

"My social circle is as small as yours. I hang out with Happy and his wife—they don't have any children—and with Jacob from work sometimes. Mostly, I work and read and go to church every time the doors open."

"And talk to your estranged wife in the middle of the night."

"Yeah," I laughed, "there's that. So… any tips on how to approach Lisa and David tomorrow?"

"Brandon, the only reason I agreed to tálk more than a few minutes with you at at your apartment was what I hope is a genuine humility on your part."

"It's real, Paula. What can I do to convince you?"

"Give it time and don't try so hard. If it's genuine…"

"You keep saying that."

"Look, I felt like a schoolgirl last Sunday night, staying up all night texting and talking to her boyfriend on the phone. According to what Pastor Hobbs and Ms. Vicki taught me from the Bible, you're the only legitimate outlet for that part of me that has been dead since you left. If it hadn't been the same for you—and I'm taking you at your word that you haven't pursued other women—I don't think you would be here."

"I wouldn't, and I promise…"

"But," she continued, holding her index finger in front her, "I need you to understand how I can't just trust my instincts. While I have enjoyed letting myself dream about what the Lord might do here, going out with you is probably not the wisest idea. Before I drove to Texas, though, I prayed some prayers that are much bigger than where I was in my new faith walk."

"I believe. Help my unbelief."

"Yes! I believe God is answering my prayers, and I further believe you are praying similar prayers. Pastor Hobbs says hope is the greatest catalyst for living out our faith here on earth. I agree with him, but everybody you meet this weekend is in place to watch my blind spots. There's quite a gauntlet in front of you over the next three days... should you choose to proceed." She added the last phrase with a sparkle in her eye that I'm sure she intended to lighten the mood after such a heavy word as *gauntlet*.

I sat back in my chair and sighed before leaning over the table to move as close as I could to Paula. "Monday at work, when I told Jacob I was coming to see you and Lisa and David, it was like he had been saving a word from the Lord for me. Happy took Roger to lunch that day so Jacob could have some one-on-one mentoring time with me."

"THAT'S SO COOL, Brandon. Mind if we veer off of our Bible study before you leave for Mississippi?" We sat in our usual corner of our favorite barbecue joint, Bibles and journals spread across the table.

"I not so sure about that. I'll need the Word more than ever this week."

"You need it in your heart more than you need it in your mind."

"True enough. What's your plan?"

Jacob fumbled with his phone for a few moments. "Write this down in your journal. It's the definition of the word *resolve*: 'firmness of purpose or intent; determination.' Got it?"

"Say it again." He did, and I wrote it down word for word. "Got it."

"Brandon, the thing that holds you back the most in your faith is doubt. Your regrets over your past, especially where it involves your family, cause you to wonder whether God can work in your life in the present. It keeps you from fully trusting Him. C.J. saw it in you. I see it. Happy sees it. And I believe that deep down inside, you understand it to be true."

I nodded, forcing myself from the urge to hang my head.

"The three of us have felt since we heard your story that God wants to do a work of restoration in your marriage. I can't tell you why I feel that way, other than the Holy Spirit speaking inside of me. We can't do it for you, but we want you to see this through for God's glory."

"Thank you. So do I. It's just..."

Jacob shook his head, scolding me. "Stop. We're going to power bomb your doubt for the next few days, starting with your memorizing the definition I just gave you while I go for a refill of sweet tea. You want some more?"

I handed him my cup as my eyes locked in on my handwritten words on the page. When Jacob returned with two full cups, I had almost committed it to memory. I expected a quiz, but he had more for me to add to my journal.

"I want you to write Romans 15:5-6 under the definition of *resolve*. It says, 'May the God of endurance and encouragement grant you to live in such harmony with one another, in accord with Christ Jesus, that together you may with one voice glorify the God and Father of our Lord Jesus Christ.' All right, buddy, commit to me that before you pack a bag for Mississippi, you'll memorize it." When I nodded, Jacob pressed, "Say it out loud."

"I will memorize the definition of resolve and Romans 15:5-6 before I pack for my trip to Mississippi."

Jacob sat back in his chair and crossed his arms. "If I know you like I think I do, you'll memorize it by tomorrow. Now, you know that song about fear being a liar that we sing so often in recovery group?"

"Love that song. It's like an anthem for me."

"Super. That's your soundtrack for this week. Play in on repeat until you're sick of it."

"This didn't take you by surprise, did it?"

He grinned. "You're not the only one praying for you and Paula and your kids to be reconciled, you know. Happy and me—we have a vested interest."

WHEN I RECITED the verses from Romans to Paula, she opened her mouth to respond, but something behind me distracted her.

"Oh, my goodness!" she exclaimed. "What are y'all doing here?"

"Date night," said an older gentleman with a refined lady beside him.

"Brandon, let me introduce you to Pastor Calvin Hobbs and his fiancee, Vicki. Calvin and Vicki, this is... my..."

"Brandon," I said, rising to meet Pastor Hobbs's handshake. "It is such an honor to meet you, sir. Paula has told me so much about how you led her to the

Lord and how both of you continue to invest in her life."

"You're not here to derail her walk with God, are you, Brandon?" he asked, still maintaining a firm grip on my hand.

"No, sir, I don't intend to do that." I maintained eye contact with him until his face softened a bit, though his eyes didn't leave mine.

Paula interrupted our stare down. "Are y'all coming or going?"

"Honey," Vicki said, "we're old folks. We eat early, go to bed early, and rise with the chickens."

"I know better than that."

"Actually, we're on our way to the Turners for game night. Y'all should join us."

"We wouldn't want to crash your party."

"Don't be silly. The more the merrier."

"You've been to game night at the Turners' house?"

"No, but you know Carol would welcome y'all to join us."

"We'll see."

"Dear, they may have more important plans," Pastor Hobbs said. "Let's leave them be. Will we see you in church Sunday morning, Brandon?" His eyes still hadn't left mine, which was disconcerting.

"If I survive the gauntlet of the rest of the weekend."

He didn't seem surprised by my response, but nodded before he and Vicki said their goodbyes and hustled toward the door. When the Hobbses were clear of earshot, I turned back to Paula. "So much for a good first impression." When she started to respond, I flashed a weak smile and waved her off. "It's fine. I'm resolved."

Paula's phone buzzed in her purse, distracting her. She pulled it out and shook her head with a grin. "I hope you didn't have any plans after dinner," she said. "It seems most of my favorite people are waiting for us at the Turners' house. Let's go."

"O-kay."

"Irv and Carol Turner."

I shrugged.

"Lonesome, party of six. They're at the Turners' house."

"*All* of them?"

"Your labyrinth just became more convoluted."

"This is not a surprise to you. You're enjoying every moment of this, aren't you?"

"Are you sweating yet?"

"I wouldn't mind stopping by my hotel to reapply deodorant."

"No time. I call being on Easton's team."

"Why? What games do y'all have planned for me?"

"Doesn't matter. I'm on Easton's team. You won't stand a chance."

18

"Paula!" exclaimed a petite brunette about ten years her senior. "You decided to join us! Come in, come in. Why, did you just finish a modeling shoot? Look at you!" She stepped back, scanning Paula from head to toe. "Why, you look gorgeous!"

A bald man I assumed to be the brunette's husband stepped over from the kitchen to join her.

"Irv, look how beautiful Paula looks tonight!"

"Hi, Paula. Dear, why don't we invite them in to join us?"

"Oh, my, where are my manners? Do come in, Paula. And who is this handsome young man you brought with you?"

"Carol, Irv, this is Brandon. Brandon, meet Irv and Carol Turner."

Irv's eager handshake confirmed the Turners were not at all shocked to find us at their door. Neither were close to a dozen folks gathered around the dining table filled with cards, dice, and board games. One of them, an older gentleman I would have guessed to be in his early eighties, walked across the room and positioned himself between Paula and me.

"My name is Jimmy Lee Yates," he began. "If I like you, I'll invite you to call me *Pops*. Until then, you can call me *sir*." I shook his hand and started to respond, but Sir was already striding back to the table.

A sharp-looking younger couple came over next. He greeted Paula with a kiss on the cheek. "Hey, sweetie."

"Watch it, pal," she responded. "You had your chance."

"If I wasn't already taken…"

"I'd hang on to this one if I was you. Hey, Sherrill."

"Hello, Paula. Great to see you again."

"Y'all, this is Brandon. Brandon, say hello to Easton Sterling and Sherill Riggs. Sherrill Riggs Sterling soon, if any of our opinions carry any weight."

Easton's hand engulfed mine as he towered over me. "On the drive over, Paula claimed you as a teammate in whatever game we play. I'm not sure what that means."

Sherrill laughed and gave Easton a push. "You might say he's a mite competitive. Only one person here can keep up with him in that regard. You claim that person as a teammate, you'll have a fighting chance. But we won't reveal who it is, right, everybody?"

When no one responded, I asked, "Sherrill, will you be on my team?"

"You got it."

Paula pulled me toward the table, where Pastor Hobbs and Vicki chatted with two girls in their twenties they introduced to me as Tara and Austen. "The Austen who started all this, I presume?" I asked, sweeping my arm across the room.

"That's me," she said with an embarrassed smile.

"Thank you for following what the Lord led you to do. Paula can't say enough about how much it meant to her and I'm assuming the rest of these folks."

"Enough with the niceties," Sir interrupted in his best attempt at gruffness. "I'm ninety-three and not getting any younger. If we're going to play games, let's get to it. It's past my bedtime already."

"You're ninety-three, Sir? I wouldn't have given you a day over eighty," I attempted.

"You knew how old I was. Don't patronize me, young fella."

"He doesn't miss a trick," I mumbled to Paula.

"His hearing's just fine, too," she whispered.

I looked up to find Sir glaring at me. "My apologies, Sir. What game were you guys playing?"

Carol clapped her hands for attention. "Tell you what, let's play an icebreaker game called Empire. We sometimes play it with our church group, and it's a fun way to introduce guests to the group. I'll be the moderator. I'll go to the foyer, and each of you will come to me one at a time and give me a fake name. It could be the name of an actual person or fictitious character—doesn't matter as long as everyone in the room will recognize the name of your character. I will add three names to the list to throw you off track. When everyone has given me their names, I'll read off the list two times only. When someone guesses who you are, you join their team, and it remains their turn. To help get to know one another, you must call the person you're guessing by his or her real name before asking. For example, if I wanted to guess who Irv is, I might say, 'Irv, are you Abraham Lincoln?' If the name he gave me is not Abraham Lincoln, it becomes Irv's turn, and he can ask anybody he wants. If he is Abraham Lincoln, then he joins my team and helps me add other people to our empire. The game keeps going until the last person is guessed. Easton and Sherrill, y'all might struggle with this, but in the end, everyone ends up on the winning team."

Sherrill laughed out loud and poked Easton in the arm. "He won't struggle with that as long as he's the head of the dynasty." He blushed and admitted it was true.

One by one, the members of the group whispered their fake names to Carol in the foyer. As I observed their interaction with one another, I found it hard to conceive that loneliness had once been their common denominator. Pastor Hobbs and his wife acted like newlyweds already. Tara and Austen interacted like long-time best friends. Easton and Sherrill could hardly keep their eyes off one another, but shared inside stories and jokes with all the others. Irv and Carol acted like hosting groups like ours was second nature. And Sir was the life of the party, swapping barbs with others a fraction of his age.

"HAS EVERYBODY GIVEN ME THEIR NAME?" Carol asked, reading through the list she had scribbled on a notepad. "I'm counting ten, plus three fake names, so that should be all of you."

"Are you not playing?" I asked.

"That wouldn't be very fair since she has the list," Sir said.

I was so embarrassed by the dumb question that I couldn't pay close attention to the list as Carol read through it the first time. In order to save myself further embarrassment, I tried to pick up several names and remember them the second time through.

"Frank Sinatra, George Jetson, the Little River Band, Happy the Dwarf, Sherrill Riggs, the Fresh Prince of Bel-Air, Pete Rose, Barney Fife, William Howard Taft, Katniss Everdeen, Annie Oakley, Billy Graham, Elizabeth Bennet, Babe Ruth."

"Who is Elizabeth Bennet?" I whispered to Paula, seated in front of me on a tall dining room chair.

"She's the main character of… uh, never mind. You'll find out later."

"O-kay, it's not that big a deal."

"Unless you're playing to win."

Carol announced, "Since Brandon is our guest, we'll let him go first. Brandon, remember to call the person's name and then ask if he or she is someone from the list. If you don't recall someone's name, you can ask for a refresher. Ready?"

Hoping to guess someone who appeared to understand the game less than I did, I asked, "Sherrill, are you Sherill Riggs?"

"Only in real life," she answered. "But for this game, no. Pops, are you William Howard Taft?"

"No. Easton, are you Pete Rose?"

"No, sir, a pitcher would never choose the all-time hits leader as his character. Tara, are you Katniss Everdeen?"

"In my dreams. Pastor Hobbs, are you Billy Graham?"

"Not in this lifetime. Austen, are you Annie Oakley?"

"No. Brandon, are you the Fresh Prince?"

"No. Irv, are you Barney Fife?"

"Yes." The group cheered as Irv took Paula's place in front of me. As Paula left, she motioned her index and middle fingers back and forth between her eyes and mine. Purposefully, I had chosen a character she would guess, which I expected she would take advantage of at her first opportunity.

"Okay, Brandon," Carol said, "since you got Irv's thinly veiled character, you get to go again. You and Irv can discuss who you want to ask."

I confessed to Irv that I didn't remember many of the names. He didn't either, so he suggested we ask one that had already been asked to pull someone with a better memory to our team. "Easton, are you Babe Ruth?"

"No. Man, even the new guy has me pigeonholed as baseball only. Are y'all accusing me of having a one track mind or something? Paula, are you Annie Oakley?"

"No. Austen, are you Elizabeth Bennet?"

"Yes."

As Austen moved to Paula's empire, Paula informed me that Miss Elizabeth Bennet was the main character in *Pride and Prejudice,* a novel by Jane *Austen.* "Were you named for her?" she asked Austen.

"My mother's a huge fan." She whispered something in Paula's ear. Paula whispered back before asking Vicki if she was Katniss Everdeen. She was not.

The game rolled on for five more minutes before Paula correctly guessed Easton as the Fresh Prince of Bel-Air, adding the teammate she most desired. When I correctly guessed Sherrill as Annie Oakley three guesses later, the battle lines became clear. Paula added Vicki as William Howard Taft, but we evened the teams by suggesting Pastor Hobbs as the Little River Band. Our side had run out of names we remembered when Paula asked Tara if she was Katniss Everdeen, whose name we had forgotten. She was not.

For our next turn, I asked, "Sir, are you Katniss?" With a grin celebrating how long he had fooled us all, he admitted he was and joined our side. Tara, as Sherrill, squared the sides at five people each, officially my team versus Paula's team. My empire could think of no other name except Billy Graham, which we figured was a fake. It was. Paula had known my character from the beginning, but everyone else had forgotten, along with her name.

With her empire gathered around her anticipating victory, Paula asked, "Brandon, are you Happy?"

"I've never been happier." Everyone applauded her team's victory as my empire crossed the room to join hers. Judging by the laughter in the room, I was not the only one enjoying the companionship and camaraderie of others. Some of them may have been accustomed to it, but I couldn't remember ever experiencing such fun outside of a bar.

Paula wrapped her arms around my right arm, squeezed, and released. "Not bad for your first round of Empire."

"Oh, so you've played this game before tonight?"

"Nope, never heard of it. Call it beginner's luck."

"Whatever you call it, I had fun meeting your friends."

"You have a big day coming up tomorrow. Want to call it a night or play another game?"

"Paula, we can stay as long as you like."

"So you really are happy?"

"This is unfamiliar territory for me—good, clean fun and all. I'm not sure what I expected from your friends, but I like them."

"I think you're making a pretty good impression on them, too."

"Almost all of them." I answered her puzzled stare, "Pops is no fan of mine."

"He is an excellent judge of character," Paula said with a playful jab to my arm. "I'm going to the kitchen for lemonade. Want some?" Before I could follow her, Easton stepped into the space Paula had vacated.

"So, Brandon, what's your intention here?"

"Here?"

"With Paula? Because if you do her wrong this time, I will gather this posse and track you down and do ugly things to you." He wasn't smiling.

"Easton, I promise, my intention is to reconcile with my family as much as they are willing."

"Convince me this change in you is authentic."

"I can give you references. You could call and talk to my boss or my pastor."

"Maybe Paula should call and talk to them."

"Maybe Paula already did."

"For real? That would be like her."

"I don't blame her. I wouldn't have trusted me as far as she did. That's what gave me hope that the Lord can restore our family. I understood what a long shot it was, but He keeps removing hurdle after hurdle."

"She still has a thing for you."

"How do you know?"

"I have two eyes. Don't mess this up, Brandon. We're praying for Paula. If you are what she thinks you are, that means we're praying for you, too. If not, well, that puts you in the crosshairs of our prayers. Just so you know."

"Thanks for caring about her, all of you. We wouldn't be on the brink of a breakthrough if all of you hadn't invested in her. I can point to several people in Texas who have done the same for me. If tomorrow goes how so many people are hoping and praying it will, we can all celebrate a miracle together."

19

I woke at dawn on Friday morning, anticipating the potential of the day. On a brisk walk through the still empty streets surrounding the hotel, I prayed for patience and for resolve. Paula was up close to the new me, but Lisa and David had only heard it secondhand from her. As I played out various scenarios in my mind, I sensed Lisa might be more easily won over since I imagined she and Paula having more intimate conversations about Paula's renewed feelings toward me. I viewed David as the harder sell. He was mister independent, army trained, more likely wary of my motives. I didn't dare come on too strong but stick with the genuine me. Give them time, the Lord kept reminding me in my spirit.

The frosty morning air and the blood pumping through my body awakened me to a nervousness that replaced my satisfaction from the previous night. I didn't tell Paula about Easton's warning or a softer one from Carol before we left game night at ten-thirty. I did tell her that Mr. Jimmy Lee had pulled me aside before he asked Tara to drive him home.

"YOUNG MAN, I give you permission to call me Pops," he declared with an air of formality after calling me toward the front door for a private conversation. "I will revoke your privilege if you ever hurt that beautiful young lady." He pointed his crooked finger toward the den where Paula was chatting with Easton and Sherrill.

"What's the deal with Paula and Easton?" I asked the man I now called Pops.

"She wasn't afraid to be frank with him about his arrogance the first time we met. He wasn't accustomed to that. When she started picking at him about Sherrill, he blushed, and she went in for the kill. They've been going back and forth ever since. It's good-natured, but she's the sandpaper he needed to rough up his perfect outer image. God was working on him already, but He used Paula to move Easton toward his breaking point. He wouldn't be the new creation he is today, nor would he be holding the hand he's holding in there right now without Paula. And Sherrill's a keeper, wouldn't you say?"

I agreed. "Paula called him as her teammate on the drive over here tonight."

Pops laughed. "Get her to tell you Easton's story sometime, and you'll understand. He's the most driven person I've ever met—too much so for his own good sometimes, but he's made a lot of progress in the last twelve months. You did good by getting Sherrill on your team during that first game. He's got nothing on her… except a ring someday soon, that is."

"I admit, I thought she gave her own name at the start of the game. Later, when I lucked up and guessed her character, I could tell that I had underestimated her. She's sharp."

"Brandon, I've seen God work more marvelous works than the one you're chasing. Paula can tell you my story, but I'm here to tell you He's powerful enough. If tomorrow doesn't go the way you hope, don't give up."

I assured him I had no plans to quit.

"Well, I see my date is ready," he said as Tara said her goodbyes and walked toward us. "Ready, good looking?" she asked Pops.

"Ready, dear," he answered, offering his arm.

She took it and turned to me. We locked eyes for an instant, her warning joining the others. "It was nice to meet you, Brandon. I hope we'll see you again."

Message received. "Nice to meet you, too. Good night. And good night to you, Pops."

He grinned, waved to the others, and stepped into the night. I found myself missing him as soon as he walked away. I told Paula about our encounter when I drove her home later.

"He's one of a kind, that's for certain. They all are, don't you think?"

I couldn't say enough positive things about the friends she had stumbled upon, and I wished I could introduce them all to Happy and C.J. and Jacob. As I walked Paula to her door, we were still laughing about what she kept referring to as the "good, clean fun" we had enjoyed.

When we reached Paula's door, I determined our fun evening wouldn't turn awkward. In the streetlight's glow, she appeared more disheveled than when we had walked out her door, but still beautiful. She might have let me kiss her, but I didn't want to complicate Friday. Instead, I reached for both of her hands, wished her a good night, and strode toward my truck before I had second thoughts. I heard her door click as I passed 4A.

"Rodney."

"Brandon."

As the sun peeked over the horizon, I sped up my pace, in part to increase blood flow on the chilly morning and because my nine o'clock breakfast appointment loomed closer. I attempted to rehearse my greetings to Lisa and David, but doubts crept in as I replayed Paula's preparation. Was she so congenial because she already knew how our children would respond to my coming to meet them? Or was she getting my spirits up in case they turned hostile? The word that continued coming to mind was *resolve.* Nothing I had experienced so far evoked the type of determination noted in the definition. What was waiting for me at Paula's place in two hours? Between the brisk pace of my walk and my nerves, the blood racing through my body warmed me as I took one more lap through the streets, which were now roaring to life.

By the time I showered and spent some time in prayer, the clock had ticked toward eight o'clock. I spent my nervous energy reading Psalm 77 out loud in order to stay focused on the words. At 8:45, my heart racing and my stomach growling, I stepped into the cab of my Happy Electric truck. My hands shook as I dropped it into gear and pulled onto the street that would take me toward my destination and my destiny. I pulled into the apartment complex at 8:55 and prayed for three solid minutes before trudging toward the stairs leading to the second floor. I passed 4A on the way.

"Rodney."

"Brandon."

"How's your day?"

"Fine."

I rapped on Paula's door at precisely 9:00. Not too early that I might seem anxious. Not a minute late to breakfast with my estranged family to hint of anything too casual. Precise, as to suggest my walking across the threshold before me was the most significant moment of my life. As soon as Paula opened the door, the scents of breakfast pushed to escape.

"Hey."

"Hey, yourself." Paula had pulled her hair back into a ponytail, and she wore gray sweatpants and a gold college hoodie. If not for the wrinkles around her eyes that showed without the previous night's makeup, one could have mistaken her for a coed.

"Are you ready?"

"As prayed up as I can be."

"Me, too. Come on in." She led the way into the den, where Lisa and David rose from the couch. She didn't mince words. "Kids, this is Brandon. He's your father."

Lisa was closest. She eased forward and stuck out a tentative hand, which I took and tried to hold. "Nice to… see you." Her hand recoiled from mine as she said it. When she stepped aside to make way for her brother, Lisa's polite smile disappeared.

"Dad," David started, testing my grip strength with his firm handshake that transitioned into the quickest of man hugs.

"Hello, David." I stared at this younger, cleaner version of myself, imagining how wiser choices at that age might have sent my life in a different direction. I wouldn't have met Paula, though, and this confident, handsome young fellow wouldn't be standing before me.

"I never saw the resemblance in you two," Paula said as David and I continued to size up one another with our right hands still locked.

I released David's hand and turned to Paula. "The last time you saw me before he was born, I wasn't clean cut like he is. I had a tough time recognizing myself under all that scruff when I had it cut and shaved. I was a shagnasty, for sure."

"A what?" Paula asked.

"It's a word Happy uses for some of the long-haired vagabonds he hires. He doesn't require much at first, but he insists that anybody in one of his trucks looks neat."

"Who's Happy?" David asked.

"Kerry Hapstead, my boss. But Happy's much more than that. He's the man who led me to Jesus, gave me a job, and continues to disciple me." Before Paula could invite us to eat breakfast, I sensed the time was appropriate for the real talk I had come to deliver. "David, Lisa—I won't beat around the bush. I did an awful thing, leaving your mother to raise the two of you. It took a lot of bad living and more than a few mistakes to open my eyes to how selfish I was. I should have been here helping raise you guys, providing for you, teaching you to ride bikes, celebrating your birthdays and graduations and all that. The regret I have over that might never go away, but I'm here today to say I'm sorry. I want to ask your forgiveness for what I've done to you and to your mother. None of you deserved this. David, son, I'm sorry for abandoning you before you were born. Words are cheap, I understand, but in your own time, I'm asking if you would forgive me and give me a second chance to be a part of your life."

My son stared through my eyes into my soul, gauging my sincerity. When my eyes held his for what seemed to me like an hour, he threw both arms around my neck. I held him in a bear hug as he shook, and I sensed years of regret transitioning into hope for our future as father and son. When he released me and pushed back to a foot from my face, his puffy eyes locked onto mine again. "I forgive you, Dad."

I thanked him, but no sound escaped my mouth. I stood holding his arms just above the elbows, still sizing him up and wondering what I could have added to his life. He didn't lack for poise or humility or resolve. That word again. "Lisa," I began, turning to my daughter at the same time the timer on the oven beeped.

"Oh, the cinnamon rolls!" Lisa exclaimed. "I forgot they were in the oven."

"I'll get them," Paula said.

"No, I've got them." Maybe I was borrowing trouble, but Lisa seemed relieved by the interruption. I followed her into the kitchen to try again after she set the steaming cinnamon rolls on top of the stove.

"Lisa..."

"Hold on, let me spread icing on top and put them back in for another minute."

I waited, exchanging a quick glance with Paula, who stood watching from the edge of the kitchen. When Lisa closed the oven and set the timer for sixty seconds, I began again.

"Lisa, I know..."

"They'll be ready in less than a minute."

Paula attempted to harness her attention. "Lisa, your father is trying to talk to you."

"I know, but these are my contribution to breakfast. I don't want them to burn."

I backed up a step toward Paula. "It's okay. I agree with Lisa—nobody likes burnt cinnamon rolls, no matter how much one might deserve one." That elicited a smile from Lisa, though I couldn't determine whether it was from my joke or the idea of feeding me such a breakfast.

A few minutes later, sausage, bacon, eggs, hash browns, and cinnamon rolls filled the small breakfast table set for four. I resolved to give Lisa a few minutes before attempting to engage her again. I passed out compliments on all the food, unsure who was responsible for each item, but not wanting to leave anyone out and risk offense. My praise for the cinnamon rolls was effusive, though I had noticed the can from which they came in the kitchen trash. Perhaps I overdid it a bit, but I couldn't stand the awkward silence coming from Lisa's direction.

"Lisa, I have something I want to say to you." This time, she stopped and sat up straight and turned her attention to me. "I want to say..."

At that, Lisa wiped the corner of her mouth with her napkin and dropped it on her plate. "I'm sorry, I can't." She rose and walked away. We heard her bedroom door close a few seconds later.

Paula attempted to reassure me. "Wait a minute. She has a lot on her mind right now, with finals and graduation and her wedding. She may have just reached overload. Give her time to sort through her thoughts."

Whatever appetites Paula, David, and I had left vanished, replaced with clumsy conversation. A few minutes passed with no Lisa. Paula stepped away from the table and disappeared around the corner. David and I eased into a discussion of his time in the military and my time skirting the law. I was frank in sharing my story with him, sure to compliment him for choosing an alternate career path. We talked easily, as much as I was able, with one ear attuned to the bedroom at the end of the hall.

Fifteen minutes after Paula left the table, she

returned, shaking her head. "I can't get her to budge. She's scared and nothing I said convinced her to hear you out. I'm sorry, but I don't know what else to do."

Resolve. It was time to exhibit the grit the Lord declared I would need. As David questioned Paula about his sister's resistance, I mouthed Romans 15:5-6: May the God of endurance and encouragement grant you to live such harmony with one another, in accord with Christ Jesus, that together you may with one voice glorify the God and Father of our Lord Jesus Christ. I added an *amen* at the end for good measure. As soon as I mouthed it, my phone buzzed with a text I had been expecting.

"Tell you what," I said, rising from the table. "I have an important errand I need to run. It will only take an hour. Maybe that'll give her enough time to change her mind. If not,..."

"No, Dad, don't go. Give me a chance to talk some sense into her."

"She has a right to whatever she's feeling. I'll be back, I promise."

Paula wasn't convinced. Following me to the door, her eyes inquired if I was running away again.

"Paula, I am resolved. I came here this weekend to give this my best shot and accept the results. I don't believe this is the end, but I understand the ground rules. If I come back in an hour and she still doesn't want to talk to me, I'll leave. That won't be the end of what the Lord is doing, I hope. I can always return if Lisa reconsiders."

"That's such a long drive."

"Not for somebody who believes he's in love." It slipped out before my filters caught it. I hadn't wanted to say it before I made peace with our children, but my heart longed for Paula. I'm not sure I had the capacity to love her before, but I did now. The time was wrong to say it, though, but I couldn't reel it back. "I'm sorry, I shouldn't have said that. Everything was going so well…"

Paula's face drooped for the briefest of moments, but she brightened and forced a smile before reaching up on her tiptoes to kiss my cheek. "Don't give up. Pray." She spun back into her apartment and closed the door behind me.

After greeting Rodney again, I re-read the text that prompted my exit.

> Just a reminder of our appointment at 10:30. Your delivery is ready for pickup.

20

Even as the sun rose near its midday peak, a wintry wind whipped through the parking lot of Paula's apartment. I withdrew as far as I could into a thin jacket, the only one I had brought with me. I tucked an envelope into an inside pocket to free up my hands to slide into the pockets. The chill was enough to drive Rodney inside, but he watched me pass 4A through a part in the blinds.

I knocked on the door of 3B. Paula's face told me all I needed to know. The sun peeking just under the edge of the roofline reflected off the moisture in her eyes. "Come in. She hasn't budged. David has been back there with her since you left, but she keeps saying that she can't, she just can't."

"Paula, I understand how difficult this is for everybody, especially Lisa. But I'm going to live up to my promise and walk away." I waved off her objection.

"This is not forever. Other times may have different ground rules—that's up to you. There's a reason Jacob gave me *resolve* as my word of the week because I'm in this for the long haul." When she didn't respond right away, I added, "Are you?"

Her pleading brown eyes met mine. "What you said about thinking you're in love… you meant that?"

"Paula, I'm sorry. I should have…"

"Don't run with it, Brandon. Answer the question."

"Yes, I mean it. I should have waited…"

"Me, too." Her hands met mine. "Please don't leave."

I breathed in the moment, imagining I would need it later. "Lisa's life is complicated right now. Let her have her moments on her terms. I wish she had responded like David did, but she's a strong young woman with the right to be herself in this. Please tell her I wish her congratulations on her graduation and nothing but the best for her wedding. She can reach out any time, and I'll be ready. We can talk about us after that. Like, *right* after that."

Paula nodded, unable to force any words as I stood. She rose with me and shuffled toward the door, glancing back toward Lisa's bedroom, hoping. When it didn't open, she hugged me and whispered, "Goodbye, Brandon."

I reached inside my jacket and withdrew a plain white envelope. "For when she's ready."

I CALLED Happy when I stopped at the red light on Highway 49 in Collins.

"Hey, Brandon. You calling with joyful news from your trip?"

"Yes and no." For the next thirty minutes, I gave Happy a play-by-play of my trip, along with the news that he could expect me at church on Sunday morning. "I'll sleep most of the day away tomorrow if I can," I said said as we wrapped up the conversation.

"And pray."

"Yeah, that's what I was doing before I called you, and it's what I'll be doing most of the drive home, I imagine." Something about the word *home* didn't land right. Harriston no longer felt like home, but neither did Texas. The cab of my truck filled with a swirl of emotions for the next hour. When I saw the Clinton exit coming up, I sensed an urge to pay Ms. Doris a visit.

I ordered the chicken sandwich meal, for which I had no appetite, while scanning the front of the restaurant for Ms. Doris. She was nowhere to be found, so I carried my tray to the corner farthest from the excited squeals emanating from the children's play area. Several bites in, my thoughts in danger of being sucked into the vortex of self-pity, the scraping of the other chair at my table scraping pulled me back.

"Brandon, right?"

"Hey, Ms. Doris. I didn't think you were working today."

"I had to give my feet a rest after the lunch rush, but this is why I take so few breaks. I sure would have hated to miss you. Your being here on Friday is not good news, am I correct? You should have come back through Clinton Sunday afternoon when we're closed. Did your wife reconsider?"

"My wife thinks she loves me, and I know I love her. I met her friends, and they gave me a stamp of approval. My son gave me a hug I'll never forget and forgave me. It's my daughter, Ms. Doris. She's the one who suggested to Paula that she set up our meeting, the one who wanted me to attend her wedding. Out of everyone whose approval I needed on this trip, she was the slam dunk."

"Until she wasn't."

"Yeah. She shook my hand hello, and something left her. I sensed it, even if I couldn't identify what changed. I'm not sure she recognizes what didn't seem right to her." Ms. Doris she listened and nodded as I filled in the details.

"What is the Lord telling you, honey?" Ms. Doris's kind steel-blue eyes beneath the silver ringlets covering her forehead invited me to share the truth with a near stranger.

"There's a guy I study the Bible with every day at work, a mentor. He gave me the word the Lord keeps reminding me of on this trip: *resolve.* It helped me push through the first steps of the gauntlet Paula had set up to test my mettle. I agreed that at any point when she or either of my children or my daughter's fiancé had reservations, I would leave. I determined to push through every door that the Lord opened and to leave without quitting if He closed one. Starting with meeting you on the drive over, the doors opened one after another until Lisa and Jake were the only ones left. I don't understand what happened, but I did what I promised Paula and God. It's just..."

"Your spirit wants to quit."

"Yes. Does that make me a failure?"

"No, honey, it makes you human. Jesus told the weary and heavy-laden to come to Him. I suspect that's why you're sitting here with me today."

"Yes, ma'am."

"Honey, I'm going to pray for you, but may I tell you a lesson I've learned and put to the test time and again in my seventy-plus years?"

"Of course."

"Brandon, like you, my spirit has screamed quit and go home at several major intersections of my life. Sometimes, my spirit rose up in me to give me the confidence that I could take on hell with a water pistol. Other times, I believe the Lord tested me to see if I would follow Him, even when I didn't feel like it. Even when it didn't make sense. That sounds like where you are now."

"Yes, ma'am, it is. People closest to me say I beat myself up too much. That's what I'm fighting against. I promise you, Ms. Doris, I will not give up. The Lord has brought me too far and worked too many—I call them miracles—to turn back now."

"You just need some encouragement."

"Yes, ma'am."

"Then let me pray for you, honey. Dear God in heaven, thank you for the difficulties you bring into our lives to draw us closer to You, to learn to trust You more. You're a wonderful Lord, mysterious and full of compassion for those who love You. This young man in front of me is in a battle to trust You when all of his circumstances haven't gone his way. Before I pray for the one that has him sitting across the table from me this afternoon, thank you for turning his wife's and his son's hearts toward him. That's Your work, Lord, and we don't want to overlook it. I pray now that you'll give him—what was that word again?"

"Resolve." The way Ms. Doris floated with ease between talking to God and to me fascinated me, and I determined to incorporate her manner into my prayers.

"Almighty God, source of every good thing we need even if we don't understand we need it, give this young man resolve. Strengthen him when he's tired and carry him when he's too weak to keep going. Restore this man's family, Lord. We'll be careful to give You the glory You deserve, because neither one of us can do what we believe is Your will in this. All blessing and honor and glory and power to You, Lord. You're worth it. We're not. Thanks again for the troubles that keep us dependent on You."

Every time it seemed Ms. Doris was bringing her prayer in for a landing, she found another aspect of my situation over which to pray. When she finished, I opened my eyes to read the intensity of her prayer through the deepened lines across her face. It was as if God had transferred the angst in my soul to her. I realized I wasn't an anomaly.

"Ms. Doris, I need to pray for you. Lord, like Isaiah

wrote, You give strength to the powerless. I can tell Ms. Doris needs a break after helping me carry my burden. Would you strengthen her for anyone else who walks through those doors needing her until—what time does your shift end?"

"Four o'clock."

"Four o'clock, then. After that, Lord, would you refresh her so she can come back to be Your hands and feet tomorrow? Thank you for putting Ms. Doris in my path, Lord."

I closed my prayer, gave her a hug, and walked toward the door.

"Brandon?" Ms. Doris called from behind me.

"Yes, ma'am?"

"Call me if you need me." She extended a simple white business card that read *Doris Clausen* on the top line, *Call me if you need me* on the second line, and her number below it. "This is my personal number. If I don't answer, I'm at work or church. Leave a message and I promise to pray for you."

"Thank you, Ms. Doris, I sure will." Again, I turned to leave.

"Brandon, one more thing."

"Yes, ma'am?"

"When God answers prayers, sometimes we forget."

"I promise to call you, Ms. Doris. You can count on it."

I walked out the door to the crisp Clinton day with an image of the pleasure on Ms. Doris's face at my response seared into my memory. "Thank you, Lord," I whispered.

As I fumbled to grab my keys from my right front pants pocket, I felt my phone buzz in the opposite pocket. I didn't recognize the number and reached to put the phone on the seat beside me. The caller gave up, and I cranked the truck for the long drive home. My phone buzzed again. Same number.

21

The silence on the other end of the phone suggested a robot call. Two seconds after my second hello, I pulled the phone from my ear to end the call.

"D-dad?"

I lurched my thumb away from the red circle. "Hello?"

"Dad, this is Lisa."

I killed the motor. "Hey, Lisa."

"Um, I wanted to call and say I'm sorry for being rude to you earlier." Her words sounded forced, not unlike a child coerced into apologizing to a sibling.

"Lisa, I understand. You have a lot on your plate right now. Perhaps this is not the right time."

"I'm graduating and getting married in three weeks, and then you came." The words were flowing now. "It's a terrible time…"

"I under—" I started.

"... to be that time of month."

"Oh. Sorry. I... should have... timed my trip better."

She chuckled. "You couldn't have known. Can you, I mean, if you don't mind—talk to me now?"

"Of course. If it's easier to talk over the phone, I want to do whatever works best for you."

"Oh." She sounded disappointed.

"Did I say something wrong?"

"No, it's just..."

"Say it, Lisa. I came prepared to face the full brunt of the crop that I've sown for the last twenty years."

"No, it's not that."

"What then? It's yours, whether you talk to me now or ever. No strings attached."

"Huh?"

"Never mind. Say what's on your mind."

"I was hoping you hadn't left Harriston yet, and maybe you'd give me another chance. In person."

"Give me two hours."

"If you're already driving..."

"I'm on my way," I said, turning the key. "Maybe less than two hours if traffic on 49 is light."

"Traffic on 49 is never light," she said. "Dad, I..."

"I'm leaving Clinton right this minute. No more arguing."

"Okay, thanks. Mom's going to cook supper here, but please don't wait until then."

"Will do," I said, turning east on Highway 80. "Lisa?"

"Yeah?"

"Did Mom give you the envelope?"

"What envelope?"

"Never mind. See you soon."

"Okay, bye."

IT WASN'T until I pulled through the light in Magee that I thought about Ms. Doris's prayer. I should have walked right back into the restaurant to update her. I pulled her card from my pocket, but the light turned green before I could punch in the numbers. As hurried as I was, I hoped the next light would be red. I breezed through Collins without slowing down, though, and thirty minutes later, the card remained untouched as I pulled into Paula's apartment complex.

I nodded at Rodney, peeking through the blinds of 4A, and mounted the stairs two at a time. The door to 3B flew open before I reached to knock, and Lisa almost knocked me down, throwing her arms around my neck.

"I love it! Thank you and I'm sorry for acting like a brat before and I'm so glad you came back!"

"Let's see you in it."

"Yes! Let me get the key."

Paula and David joined me as Lisa skipped to the slate blue sedan that Richardson Motors had delivered to Harriston earlier Friday morning. Paula and I stood behind the car as Lisa hopped into the driver's seat and David into the passenger's side. She slipped her arm around my waist. "This way worked out much better."

My arm swung up toward Paula's shoulder, but when she released my waist, I scratched my ear that didn't itch instead. "What do you mean?"

"She did not know about the car. Neither did I, so I didn't influence her calling you either."

"What happened?"

"She said your being here, along with everything else going on in her life, overwhelmed her. Then, she felt she had dug a hole too deep to climb out of and she froze. She'll tell you when y'all go for a drive, I'm sure. Go take her picture in her car."

I pulled out my phone and opened the camera app. Lisa and David were talking inside the car, so I tapped on Lisa's window and beckoned her to let down her window. When she did, I had her assume a dozen different poses and snapped photo after photo with my camera and hers. I asked if she had driven it yet, and she stopped smiling.

"No. I thought I might take you for a drive and talk if that's okay?"

"Sure. Should I take the backseat or kick David out?"

"Just us, if that's okay."

"Fine with me."

As I walked around the car, David met me and whispered, "It'll be okay."

I sniffed the new car smell that still lingered in the two-year-old sedan, an aroma that I enjoyed in my new work truck. "It's not brand new, but I hope it will last you a long time."

Lisa reached for the ignition and stopped. "Dad, I

didn't know about the car before I called. Mom didn't even realize you had bought it and brought it here."

"Let me say up front that this car is not a means to buy your favor. I prayed long and hard about buying it, and the Lord impressed on me that if I could give it to you without expecting your forgiveness or anything else, I should buy the car."

"But how did you... I mean, wasn't it expensive?"

"I had been saving for a while to buy my own vehicle. My boss lets me drive my work truck everywhere I go, though, and he gave me a new truck last week."

"That's cool."

"He's cool. His name is Kerry Hapstead, but everybody calls him Happy. That's why the company is called Happy Electric. I've been working my way up in the company, and even though I'm not making a ton of money, I'm a contributing member of society, something I haven't been in a long time. You should have a reliable car as a wedding gift. I had no guarantee I would pass all the tests laid out for me this weekend, so I had it delivered with no reservations about leaving it if y'all sent me packing."

"Which I almost did. I'm sorry."

"No need to apologize. You had every right to react however you saw fit. I'm glad you changed your mind, though. Enough about me, though, you mom tells me you'll be graduating in December and getting married the same day."

"Yeah," Lisa said, cranking the car and backing cautiously out of her parking spot. She turned onto 28th Avenue and drove toward the college campus. "You'll meet Jake tonight. He's sweet. I don't think I could have met anyone more meant for me. I hope you like him."

"I'm sure I will. How's the car driving?"

"Super smooth. I can't even hear the engine," she said, smiling and glancing toward me, but not taking her eyes off the road. Lisa turned onto the campus and gave me a quick tour that focused on the buildings where she attended various classes. She recalled Paula selling their house to move closer to campus so they could buy one dependable car and live close enough for Lisa to walk to school. She scheduled her first class to coincide with Jake's now so she could ride to campus with him. When she pulled into a parking space in front of a building she identified as her home away from home, she pointed to a live oak consuming the space between it and the nursing building.

"See that tree?"

"Yeah, it looks like a kid's playground," I said, referring to the sprawling lower branches that beckoned one to climb.

Lisa grinned. "Come on, let me show you."

We exited the car, and she led me to the side opposite us, where someone had propped a crude, three-step ladder against the base of the tree. Lisa bounced up the ladder as if she had done it hundreds of times and beckoned me to follow her onto the first branch. I moved a little slower, trying to balance myself as I followed her halfway out onto the branch, where she sat and waited for me.

"Look," she said, pointing to a spot beside her left leg. When I sat on the limb, my eyes found the initials

JNLG carved into the wood. "Jake Noble, Lisa Gull. Jake did that on the two-year anniversary of our first date. This is where we ate lunch and talked most days. It has been our private place amid thousands of people milling around campus, like our little sanctuary. This is where I fell in love with him."

"Thank you for bringing me here."

"Dad?"

"Yes?"

"I fell in love in the wrong order."

"What do you mean?"

"A girl should fall in love with her daddy first."

I hung my head, muttering *resolve* in my mind as I prepared for the onslaught I deserved and half expected from Lisa, David, or Paula on this trip. I forced my eyes to meet hers. Moisture clung to mine.

"I think I intuitively understood that but didn't know how to put words to it. But then I've watched Mom since she spent Thanksgiving without us last year. David and I were both concerned about her. When I came back from meeting Jake's family that weekend, I prepared to walk on eggshells around Mom to give her time to adjust to the thought of my leaving home this year. She had this vitality about her, though, that I didn't ask her to explain at first. It carried over through Christmas without David and into the new year. I figured it was related to the people she met at Thanksgiving, but life went on for months after that, and I never mentioned it. Still, I had little doubt something significant in her had changed.

"Let me back up and say that Jake and I keep a

standing date on Sundays, from whenever we feel like getting up through lunch when we don't do any schoolwork. We start early most weeks so we can spend as much school-free time together as possible. He picks me up around seven and takes me to a coffee shop we like for coffee and beignets. Sometimes we meet some of our friends for church, but most times we sit there talking all morning or go to the park for a walk or something like that. One morning in early summer, we were planning to meet up with friends for church, but I was attacked by powdered sugar. If you've ever eaten beignets, you understand what I'm talking about."

I nodded, feeling a sudden craving for the New Orleans delicacy. Perhaps Paula would be interested in joining Jake and Lisa and me for coffee and beignets early Sunday morning… if I was still in Harriston by then.

"We ran by the apartment to change tops, and Mom wasn't home. I thought nothing of it then. I figured she had gone grocery shopping or something like that. After Jake left that night, she asked about my day, and I told her about the sugar explosion and returning to the apartment to change. When I said I figured she was out grocery shopping, I noticed her flinch. My first thought was *oh my gosh, does my mother have a boyfriend*? I raised my eyebrow and asked if there was something she needed to tell me. That's when she told me about going to see Pastor Hobbs, who led her to Jesus."

"Seems like a fine man."

"She told me she had given her life to God and that the reason she wasn't home was because she had been attending his church out in the country. I asked why she hadn't told me, and she responded that she had been trying to muster the courage to tell me. It struck me as odd that she would need courage to tell me something that important to her, so I asked more probing questions."

"What did she tell you?"

"That she was still trying to figure out what it meant. It represented such a change for her that she could hardly put it into words, which still didn't make sense to me. Not long after we talked, though, David returned from Iraq, and I forgot about diving deeper into what had happened to Mom. Turns out, she was attempting to track down somebody and didn't want to tell either of us about just yet. "

"Me."

"Yeah. Well, it all came out at Thanksgiving. Their group from last year—they call themselves Lonesome, party of six—met for dessert Thanksgiving night. It was neat. They all brought family or friends and told how their lives had differed from the year before. Mom started talking and I guess she forgot David and I were in the room, but she told the entire story of how she found you. When she went through the police reports and the things you had done, I figured that was the end of whatever she was attempting to accomplish. It surprised David as much as it did me when she came to find you, but her reason shocked us. That's when I understood the change I saw in Mom was genuine.

"As Mom shared what the two of you discussed, I felt Jake reach for my left hand. I took it, but then I realized Jake was sitting to my right. It was David who had reached for me. He was hanging on every word she was saying. Mom doesn't know how often David and I discussed what it might be like to find you one day. Never in our wildest dreams did we imagine Mom's reaching out to you. I said nothing to David, but I figured she must have overheard one of our conversations and reached out to you on our behalf. That wasn't true, either.

"When you took my hand, it flashed across my mind that seeing that right in from of her might hurt Mom. And then I froze. I have so much going on, and with—you know, my monthly visitor—I just locked up. Mom tried to bring me to my senses, but I wanted everything to return to the way it was before all this. She gave up, but David didn't. I wouldn't listen to him at first, but he reached to take my hand, which took me back to Thanksgiving night when we were so hopeful about a relationship with you. I finally opened up and told David about my fear of hurting Mom. He said, 'Lisa, are you blind?' I was like, 'Huh?' And he said, 'I think Mom is still in love with Dad.' When I didn't filter it through my own insecurities, I saw he was right. But you were already gone."

I shifted my weight on the enormous live oak limb to keep my feet from falling asleep and to look at my daughter square in the face. "Lisa, my greatest regret in life is abandoning your mom and you and David. An apology can't make amends for the years I threw away and the responsibilities I have shirked. That said, I am deeply and truly sorry, and I take responsibility for my actions. If you could find it in your heart to forgive me, I'll spend the rest of my life doing my best to make it up to you."

In a broken voice just above a whisper, my daughter offered forgiveness and melted into my arms.

22

Lisa pulled back and repositioned herself. Sitting on a tree branch in front of an academic building on a college campus seemed as natural to her as my sitting in Happy's office. I pointed to the JNLG carved into the wood. "You say this was where you fell in love with Jake?"

"Yeah, right here."

"What made you realize you were in love with him?"

"How personal shall I be?"

"You've heard my story, and it's no prize. You can tell me anything."

"Okay, but you can't unhear what I'm about to tell you."

I braced myself. "Go ahead. These are the times I should have been present while you were growing up, so I won't shy away from them now."

Lisa's eyes fell to her lap, where her hands twitched.

"When Jake and I first started dating, neither of us had ever been involved in a serious relationship. We had asked friends to be our dates to school events and stuff like that, but we didn't understand how an actual relationship worked. I was too quick to share my inner feelings and struggles with him, and he was—still is—an awesome listener. But, I guess because we moved too fast toward sharing our intimate feelings with one another and that led to… Dad, we messed up."

"I'm sorry." My arm around her shoulders seemed to suffice for words I couldn't produce.

"This is college, so our classmates don't exactly frown upon having sex. But it didn't seem right to me, and I couldn't focus on anything else the next day. I skipped my business management class the next day, the only class I've ever missed during college. Jake was in the class, too, and I couldn't face him. I tried to push through—attempted to convince myself that it was no big deal. It was, though, and I walked from our apartment to here to sit and think. Halfway through that class period, I saw Jake leaving the business building. Even from that distance, he seemed troubled, like I was, and I wanted to call his name. It turned out I didn't need to because he glanced this way and spotted me in the tree. He climbed up beside me and sat without a word for the longest time."

"LISA, I'M SORRY."

"Should we be sorry for… you know."

"Calling it *you know* might be an indication."

"But I don't want to lose you, Jake."

Jake sat without speaking for so long that Lisa braced herself for a breakup.

"Lisa, I knew better."

"What do you mean?"

"I'm not sure I can say this without offending you."

"Since I have no idea what you're talking about, please just say what's on your mind."

"I… come from… a family with… a strong father." His words rushed like water from a broken levee after that. "I'm not judging you for not having a dad, because that's not your fault. My dad had 'the talk' with me, though, and my parents are Christians who warned me about the consequences of sex before marriage. I suspected they were speaking from experience, but nobody wants to ask their parents about that. Anyway, I listened and agreed with them, but our conversation was so… sterile. It didn't involve… you… or…"

"Or what?"

Jake sighed and lamented, "Ideally, I would have come over to pick you up the first time. Your dad would have been sitting in the den cleaning his gun or sharpening his machete or something cliché like that. It would have worked, too, because it would have reminded me of how I should act around the woman I…" He stopped and looked down.

"So what do we do now?"

"I came up with a plan, but you may not agree with it."

"If it will make the churning inside me go away…"

"Oh, my gosh, Lisa, don't say that."

"Please, God, no," Lisa whispered before turning her attention back to Jake. "If it will make the knots in my stomach go away, I'm all ears."

"I wish I could undo last night, but the best I can do is make sure we wait until… I mean, look at how it's affecting both of us. Clearly, we weren't ready for that step. I'm sorry for not taking the lead the way I should have."

"It was both of us, Jake. I could have stopped you, but I didn't. I thought it was something I wanted, but… you won't take offense that I regret it?"

"No, not at all. Gosh, no. But I want to ask for a second chance to—like my dad would say—live up to my name. You know, Noble."

"But how? That say that once you've taken that step…"

"Who's *they*? I think we should listen less to *they* and more to *us*. We're not bound by what some all-knowing council of *they* say."

"I'm listening."

"Lisa, I'm asking you for permission to share this with my dad."

"Oh, no, Jake, that…"

"Hear me out. My dad is a vault when it comes to sharing personal issues. I've done it before, and I promise we can trust him. Something like this—he wouldn't even share it with Mom."

"I don't know, Jake. If I ever met him, it would be weird—his knowing and my knowing that he knows."

"I don't trust myself, though, and this is too important. Lisa, I..."

"That's the third time you've started to say something and stopped. What is it you're not telling me?"

Jake turned to straddle the limb and stared directly into Lisa's eyes. "Lisa, I love you. Not because of last night. But I will love you enough to stay pure from now until our wedding night. It's going to be more difficult now, and I don't want to mess it up. There, I said it, and I'll say it again. I love you, and I plan to marry you one day."

"THAT'S the moment I realized I loved him, Dad. It wasn't when he told me he loved me, and it certainly wasn't when we had sex. I saw his willingness to humble himself for me, kind of like I'm watching you do with our family. Dad?"

"Yes?"

"I'm scared. We didn't go to church much growing up, other than vacation Bible schools during the summer. David and I always felt like those were to give Mom a break from us. Jake grew up going to church every time the doors opened, to borrow a cliché. I don't want to tell Jake or Mom, but what if Jake and me end up..."

"Like your mom and me?"

Lisa hung her head. "Yeah. I'm sorry. I'm new to this marriage thing."

"You won't."

She raised her eyes to meet mine. "How can you be sure?"

"I can't. But if Jake is everything you say, he is many times the man I was at his age or than I've ever been. Did you give him permission to talk to his dad?"

"I did, and it was fine. Mr. Noble didn't act funny toward me at all."

"I'm glad."

"Dad?"

"Yeah?"

"When did you recognize you were in love with Mom?"

Of all the scenarios I had played out in my head before, during, and after my drive to Mississippi, this question was never a part of one of them. I hesitated, unsure why Lisa asked. Was she curious, just making conversation? Or was she asking for confirmation as she approached her wedding day? It was a tough question, one for which I didn't have a ready answer. I bought time by squirming into a more comfortable position.

"Like super infatuated with her, or the type of love you just described between you and Jake?"

"That one."

"Last night."

Her arched eyes said it wasn't the answer she imagined. With as much economy of words as I could muster, I took Lisa from the first time I laid eyes on Paula at Jimmy's Bar and Grill to our all-night phone call five days earlier.

"I have been praying since I gave my life to Jesus for reconciliation with your mom and you and David. I thought it would be an incredible answer to prayer if I could apologize with none of you taking my head clean off. My boss, Happy, has been praying for much more than an apology and forgiveness, though. He didn't reveal the extent of what he believes God wants to do until Sunday afternoon. When he told me he thought God wanted to restore my marriage with your mother, something inside of me that didn't want to speak up woke up and hoped for a miracle. When I sent your mom a text in the middle of the night by accident and she answered it, I saw it begin to unfold. I cautioned myself not to read too much into our conversation, but I felt like something bigger than either of us was orchestrating our lives toward one another."

I told Lisa about finding a restaurant in Clinton that was farther off the interstate than I had intended and how I met Ms. Doris there. For a second time, I sensed the pangs of guilt at not calling and giving her the news that God had resurrected my weekend with my family.

"When I arrived at your mom's place and passed her security guard…"

"4A?"

"Yeah. Rodney and I are old pals now."

"That's funny."

"Anyway, when your mom answered the door, this incredible surge of… something ran through me. Except for her trip to Texas, I hadn't seen her in twenty years, and that meeting was such a blur that it almost doesn't count. We talked for a while, and the time came for me to check into my hotel and get ready for our dinner meeting to discuss the plans to meet with you and

David. I asked what she was wearing, and she seemed excited to be going to a fancy restaurant with me. I shouldn't have, but as I was walking out, I asked her if this was a date. She said 'we'll see,' but the way she said it released a swarm of butterflies in my stomach. When I picked her up, she brought it back up, and we agreed to call it like an awkward first date on which we would talk about our grown children."

"You were nervous?"

"Oh, my goodness, yes. First off, Paula was stunning, and I felt outclassed, especially when we pulled into the parking lot full of fancy cars in my Happy Electric work truck."

"Your *new* truck."

"Yeah, but I don't imagine the people in the fancy cars were saying to themselves, *boy, check out that brand new work truck.*"

"Okay, you're right. That's the first time you've called Mom *Paula* instead of *your mom*. You should stick with that. Go on."

"So we walk through the parking lot, and your mom —Paula—suggests we pretend we came in this sporty black Audi."

"She named it, too, didn't she?"

"Yes!"

"I don't know where she picked that up, probably in some book she read. What did she name this one?"

"Marguerite."

"Fancy. I haven't heard her use that one. Keep going."

"By the time we strolled into the restaurant, my

mind had adjusted to this being an actual date instead of a pretend one. I couldn't keep my eyes off Paula. I'm not sure what I expected, but her life has been so difficult..."

"That you expected her to be living under a bridge."

"Perhaps not quite that destitute, but you get the picture. Lisa, I'm telling you, she was the class of the place. The way she carried herself—it's hard to put into words. And there she sat, across the table from the guy who least deserved to be sitting there."

"That's the change in her I was telling you about earlier. Did she tell you about her outfit?"

"Yeah. Gifted dress, borrowed boots, Goodwill scarf. You would have thought she had one of those personal shoppers pick out everything for her. Just when I settled into a groove for our date that I hadn't expected to be one, she pulled the rug out from under my feet."

"What do you mean?"

"She laid out the schedule she had planned for the weekend. She was blunt about this entire weekend being over if any of you nixed it, and I agreed. That was the context I expected from our dinner from the beginning, but it did kind of put a damper on the idea of its being an actual date. Still, Paula carried a determination and spunk that was attractive to me. When she said she was praying y'all would expose me if I wasn't willing to see this through, my resolve to obey God only grew stronger. And then, she told me she was pulling for me. Until she said that, I hadn't allowed myself to believe that our getting back together was realistic. That's when I admitted to myself that I love my wife. Whether I did twenty years ago, I can't say. Perhaps we both needed to give our lives to God before we could think about giving them back to one another. I can tell you I am in love with your mother, though. I haven't said that out loud to anybody except you."

Lisa sat without speaking for a solid minute. She raised her head and locked eyes with me. This time, moisture clouded her gaze. "I almost cost you guys a chance at that."

"Quit beating yourself up over that. Your mom—sorry, Paula—said it was better this way. You made your choices on your own before you found out about the car."

"Dad?"

"Yes?"

"I'm going to tell you something."

"Anything."

"I want to say it once while we're sitting here in my favorite place and grow into it over time other places."

"Go for it."

My daughter reached for my hands and squeezed them. "I love you, Dad."

23

When Lisa and I walked back into the apartment two hours after we left it, the aroma of dinner cooking alerted me I was famished. No one acted surprised that Lisa's spin in her new car took as long as it did. She bounced across the living area to her room to freshen up before Jake arrived.

"I guess she liked it?" Paula asked from the kitchen, where steam from a large pot on the stove threatened to engulf her.

"Huh?"

"The car."

"Oh, yeah, she said she could hardly hear it running."

"Mine has a knock I've been meaning to get checked out, but I was hoping to put it off until after the wedding. Good thing I'll be arriving at the wedding venue early, so my jalopy won't embarrass me."

"I could take you in my fine Happy Electric-mobile.

It wouldn't be the first time you've dressed nice for a ride in a work truck."

Paula shook her head and motioned me to join her in the kitchen. "I wouldn't mind. So if you're coming to the wedding, I guess you and Lisa talked?"

"We did."

"And?"

"I'm coming to the wedding."

"That's it?"

"Lisa is more than I could have imagined in someone who shares my DNA. Paula, how did you raise such incredible children?"

"It wasn't easy."

"I know."

"Stop."

"Stop what?"

"You're trying to visit that place where you beat yourself up again. I'm assuming Lisa forgave you when you asked?"

"And then some."

"That's all of us, then. If I can talk about the lost years without anger, can you talk about them without shame?"

"I want to, but I don't want it to appear that I'm showing up after twenty years with a flippant 'oh, my bad about the whole walking out on you guys' thing."

Paula turned from stirring noodles to plant her hands on my shoulders. "If any of us believed that, your skinny butt would already be back in Texas. I'll tell you how the kids and I survived. We moved forward. I was mad at you for the first few years… okay, first couple of decades. When Lisa and then David started school, I poured myself into Lisa's education and David's business. They set their hearts there, so I did everything I could to help them pursue their dreams. When life knocked one of us down, the other two pulled the other one up, and we kept moving. Looking back, I recognize that what I couldn't give them financially, we provided one another in determination and resilience."

"I see that."

She stirred a boiler of what appeared to be spaghetti sauce before returning her attention to me. "Brandon, I want you to realize we would have been better off with you here. Just because Lisa and David are remarkable people doesn't mean they don't have their wounds. They needed you. They still need you."

"And you needed me."

"I…"

A knock on the door interrupted our conversation.

"That must be Jake. Will you answer the door?"

"What if it's Rodney?"

Paula slapped my arm. "Don't start. The kids give me enough grief about having a thing for him."

I had hoped to check back into my hotel and change into some fresh clothes before dinner, but my rumpled shirt would have to do. I opened the door and stood face to face with a bookish-looking young man in khakis and a white button-down and holding a bouquet of fall flowers. "Jake, I presume?"

"Yes, sir."

"Brandon." I extended my hand, and he took it with a grip stronger than I expected. He maintained eye contact through the handshake, and I liked him right away. "Come on in."

"Hey, Jake," Paula called from the kitchen.

"Hey, Paula. How are you?"

"Fine. How was your day?"

"Busy. I brought some flowers for… well, I guess they're for everybody."

"That was sweet of you. Here, let me find a vase."

While Paula fluffed up the bouquet to fit the vase, Lisa floated into the room in jeans and a white sweatshirt with a red-nosed reindeer that proclaimed *Merry Christmas*. "Hey, Jake," she greeted him with a hug.

"Hey, you."

"You met my dad?"

"Yes."

"Want to go for a walk?" I noticed the nudge she gave him.

"Uh, sure. How long until supper?"

Paula looked to the ceiling for answers. "Let's see, the sauce and green beans are ready. The noodles won't take long. Oh, I need to put the bread in the oven."

"Twenty minutes," said David, appearing from the hallway. "Mom has never given a straight answer to the how long until dinner question. Hey, Dad."

"Hey."

"Enough picking on Paula time," Paula called across the kitchen. "Lisa, you and Jake go for your walk and be back in time for supper." Turning to David and me, she said, "And you two find something to do to stay out of my kitchen. Too many cooks and all."

"Hey, I need to run an errand," I said.

"A less-than-twenty-minutes errand?"

"Yes. David, want to ride with me?"

"Sure. There you go, Mom. Just you and the kitchen. Don't blow it."

"Nineteen minutes. Get moving."

SEVENTEEN MINUTES LATER, I pulled back into the parking lot. David and I exited my truck as Lisa and Jake turned the corner, so we waited for them and walked to the stairs together, past 4A.

"Rodney."

"Brandon."

As soon as the door closed behind us, the kids burst out laughing.

"Dad, you weren't kidding when you said you've met Rodney," Lisa said, clutching her side.

"Oh, Rodney and I are old pals."

"Mom has a crush on him, you know."

"So I've heard. You should have seen his face when Mom introduced me to him as her husband."

"I do not have a crush on Creepy Rodney!" Paula protested from the kitchen.

"Who's your crush, then?" Lisa asked as Jake joined her in the dining area adjacent to the kitchen.

"For me to know and you to find out," Paula answered with a coy smile.

"What, are you in third grade? Come on, Mom, share with the class."

I feigned interest in a book lying on the coffee table

while Lisa prodded her mother. David sat on the couch beside me, inspecting the spine of the book that covered the grin on my face.

"I'm too old for crushes."

David joined the fray. "Are you now?"

"What's with you, anyway? Have you and your father been out drinking?"

"No!" we exclaimed together before I returned to my book.

"You act like it. Wash up, everybody. The bread needs two minutes."

"What are we having again?" I asked.

"Do what I told you, and you'll find out soon enough."

"Ouch," David said. "Guess you better mind, Dad, or she might make you go hungry."

I obediently walked down the hall to wash my hands, as did Lisa and David. "Stop picking at your mother, Lisa. I, for one, appreciate her cooking supper for us all. The last time I ate supper with you was when you were in a high chair."

"Oh, come on, Dad, don't you want to hear Mom say she's crushing on you?"

"What are y'all talking about?" David asked.

"Dad's in love with Mom," Lisa said with a teasing grin before flicking water in my face.

"I guess y'all had a pleasant enough talk, then?"

"Yeah, he passed. And he's in love with our mother."

David looked into my eyes, more serious than his sister and almost melancholy. "Are you planning to stay in our lives for keeps?"

Caught in between Lisa's playfulness, David's sad countenance, and Paula's pleas to come to the table, I pulled both children close and turned to David. "I believe the Lord is at work in our family. When I left you guys so long ago, I had no idea what genuine love was. Now that I do, I see you all differently, and I will do whatever it takes to be a part of your lives." Peering into David's eyes, I added, "For keeps." I told Lisa, "If your mother feels it, too, let her say it herself and in her own timing, okay?"

We squeezed three wide up the hall toward the dining area, my arms still around them. I released Lisa to Jake, who held her chair for her. They squeezed into one side of the table built for four. David sat opposite them, so I took the chair farthest from the kitchen. No sooner had I sat, Paula called me to the kitchen to help serve. She had heaped spaghetti on each of the five plates, along with two pieces of whole grain bread. She was spooning green beans onto the plates when I walked up behind her.

"Here, take the forks and napkins first." She avoided eye contact when she gave the orders and when handed me the plates to the table.

"Ooh, what's that I smell?"

"Dessert."

"What is it? It smells delicious."

"You'll find out soon enough."

Lisa called into the kitchen, "Mom, is that any way to talk to your guest?"

I had a hunch it was apple pie. I tested my theory when we had all gathered at the table. After David asked God to bless our food, I said, "Great choice on the food, Paula. I haven't eaten spaghetti in months. You wouldn't happen to have any..."

She turned and reached for a grocery bag sitting on the counter separating the dining area from the kitchen. She pulled out a bottle of habanero sauce and slid it across the table to me.

"You remembered. Thank you." I held her gaze.

Lisa's eyes flashed back and forth between us. "Wait, what just happened?"

"Your father always enjoyed a splash or two of habanero sauce mixed in with his spaghetti, that's all."

"No, that's not all. Why do y'all...?"

My eyes remained locked on Paula's. "That's an apple pie in the oven, isn't it?"

Paula blushed, and Lisa noticed. "Mom?"

"Ooh, I almost forgot," Paula said, jumping up from the table and returning to the kitchen. She returned with two candlesticks and a lighter. After placing the candles on the table, she met my eyes. "Brandon, you want to do the honors?"

"Sure." I rose and took the lighter from her, but when I did, our hands touched. Neither of us moved for a few seconds.

"Come on," Lisa said, exasperated. "What are y'all not telling us?"

I spoke first. "Lisa, David, Jake—your mother has re-created the meal, candles included, that she cooked for me when she broke the news that we were going to have a baby."

"We won't talk about the first time I tried to tell

him," Paula said. She appeared to regret adding the memory we would both like to forget.

"Yes, we will," I countered. "Rip off the bandaid and tell them the rest of the story."

Paula seemed reluctant to tell them about packing a picnic for two with plans to share her exciting news with me at the lake, only to find my friends and their beer waiting for us there. When she reached the end of her abridged version of the story, I pulled back from the table and made for the front door.

"Brandon, where are you going? I thought you wanted me to tell it."

"Let him go," David said when Paula rose to follow me to the door.

Two minutes later, I marched back through the door holding two bottles of sparkling grape juice. Paula's hands involuntarily covered her mouth. "Paula, we can't go back and undo the past, but perhaps we can redeem a not-so-insignificant part of it?"

Paula nodded and brought five mismatched glasses from the kitchen, which I filled. When we had both returned to our dinner, Paula caught David staring at her. "You knew about this, didn't you, son?"

"Not exactly. Dad told me not to tell y'all he bought it, but I figured he wanted to surprise you later. When you told how he embarrassed you in front of his friends for bringing a non-alcoholic drink to the picnic, I connected the dots. Well played, Dad."

After we finished dinner and carried our dishes to the kitchen, where Paula said Lisa would clean them later, we moved to the living room. Joining Jake and Lisa on the couch, while Paula and David sat in armchairs on either side of us, I felt at home. The fear that the other shoe could drop at any time was finally gone. I longed to stay for more than two more days.

I asked David more questions about his experience serving our country, and he recounted several stories. After he had talked for a while, I prompted Lisa to share how one elementary teacher inspired in her a love of learning that led her to scholarships and college and, soon, graduation. Even though I knew much of the story, I had Jake lay out his plan to propose to Lisa. I was about to have Paula share her experience of the week at the beach she had longed for so long when a random thought ran across my brain.

"Oh, my goodness, I cancelled my hotel room and didn't re-book." With so much activity piled into one afternoon and evening, calling the hotel had slipped my mind. At a few minutes after ten, I reached for my phone to book a room at the same hotel.

"You can stay at my place," Jake interrupted. He hadn't offered more than a few words at our family reunion.

"No, I don't want to inconvenience you."

"It's no trouble. My roommate moved out last week. He and his fiancée are hotel and restaurant majors who started their empire by purchasing a duplex near campus. They'll live on one side and rent out the other. When they got far enough along on the renovation two weekends ago, he moved over there to cut down on his commute. Anyway, he found a great deal on a used bedroom suite, so his old bed is still at our apartment, clean sheets and everything. You're welcome to it."

"Okay, I'll take you up on the offer."

"We don't have much to eat."

"We'll take care of meals here," Paula said. "If you'll grab something for breakfast, we'll do lunch here—sandwiches and chips, if that's okay. I thought we might all go out to eat somewhere nice tomorrow night."

"My treat," David insisted.

"About breakfast, I heard there was a neat spot where they serve incredible beignets and coffee."

"Ah, someone's been getting recommendations from Lisa," Paula said.

"I have, indeed. She said their beignets were the key to solving the mystery of where you had been slipping off to on Sunday mornings."

"Guilty."

"After such an eventful day today, I wondered if you might want to meet me there at 7:00 in the morning to debrief."

"I sleep in as long as I can on Saturdays."

"Mom!" Lisa exclaimed. "Can't you tell Dad is asking you out? You keep being rude to him." Turning to face me, she continued, "Dad, I understand you've been out of the dating arena for a minute, but *debrief* is not an enticing word to use when asking a girl for a date."

"How would you have worded it, Miss Smarty Pants?"

"Hmm, let me think. Perhaps *Paula, even with all the time we've spent together these last two days, I just can't get enough of you. Want to throw your hair in a ponytail and go out for the best beignets and coffee on the planet tomorrow morning?* Oh, and you might throw in an *I'll pick you up* instead of *meet me there.*"

Paula shook her head in amusement at Lisa. "I don't know what's gotten into you, but you're full of yourself tonight. Quit picking at your father. He's had a long day."

"Paula," I began before the opportunity passed, "even with all the time we've spent together these last two days, I just can't get enough of you. Want to throw your hair in a ponytail and go out for the best beignets and coffee on the planet tomorrow morning? I'll pick you up in the Happy-mobile."

"The Happy-mobile, is it?"

"Marguerite is in the shop."

"Stop it."

"Well, Mom?" Lisa asked, not about to allow her to change the subject without a definitive answer. "Dad's waiting."

"Sure, I'll go for beignets and coffee with you in the Happy-mobile tomorrow morning."

"Finish it."

"What?"

"Say *it's a date.*"

Paula swiped at hair that wasn't dangling in her face. "Fine, it's a date. There, you happy?"

Lisa snuggled against Jake's shoulder. "I am. I'm happier than the little smiley man on Dad's truck."

"That's the Happy-mobile to you," I said.

"I think you should be the happy one," she shot back. "It's not every day a guy gets a date with a woman of Mom's caliber."

"You couldn't be more correct, Miss Matchmaker. Should I tell Rodney or let his heart break when he sees us leaving together tomorrow morning?"

"Oh, he'll see us," Paula said. "Creepy Rodney doesn't miss a thing. I don't believe the man sleeps."

"HAPPY, I'M OVERWHELMED," I summarized after bringing my friend up to speed on the events of my Friday on the drive to Jake's apartment later. "This many positive things didn't happen to me in twenty years, much less in a weekend."

"No, you're right, it doesn't. Unless God is working a miracle, that is. With Him, all things are possible."

"Has he ever rained down these kinds of blessings on you?"

"Every time I come across a lost sheep, and the Lord uses me to bring him into the fold. Salvation is the biggest miracle, Brandon. We can't make that happen, only God's Spirit. Restoring your relationships like He's doing still pales compared to bringing the spiritually dead to life, remember that. Since you and Paula have both experienced that miracle—and recently, at that—you can both believe Him for something less, however crazy it might seem."

"It sure doesn't feel like less, Happy."

"Tell me then—when did this entire chain of events begin?"

"When He saved us, I guess."

"There you go. Good night, Brandon. Tell Paula I said hello."

24

"Good morning, Rodney."

"Brandon."

"How are you doing this beautiful day?"

"Fine."

"Any plans today?"

"No."

"I have a date with Paula this morning."

"Okay."

"Well, good talk, Rodney. I hope you have a tremendous day. I'm going to pick up my date now."

"Bye."

I KNOCKED on 3B wearing jeans and a heather gray Happy Electric sweatshirt, figuring Paula would choose similar garb. When she opened the door wearing a simple but stylish black top with a maroon skirt and with her hair styled, I looked the part of a vagabond.

"Good morning, Brandon."

"Good morning, yourself. Wow, you look amazing."

She twirled around, fluffing her skirt as she did. "You like?"

"Yeah, but I seem, uh, unprepared."

"It's okay, I'll change. Lisa gave me free rein of her closet, so I've been enjoying trying on dress-up clothes for more than church."

"I would tell you I'd grab a dressier shirt and some other shoes from my truck, but I don't imagine that black shirt would mix well with powdered sugar."

"No, I suppose it wouldn't. I wasn't going to wear this, but I thought I'd surprise you when you showed up this morning and see your response. You think it looks okay? I'm thinking about wearing it tonight. "

"Classy, like Thursday night."

"Lisa has a taste for classy clothes that most girls don't. I'm her beneficiary."

"Maybe you should go shopping with her before she moves out."

"Oh, I can't afford some things she buys. All this eating at fancy restaurants and wearing nice clothes is not how we live day in and day out. We'll go back to normal on Monday, but I figured I would enjoy some higher class living for a few days. I could get used to eating out, dressing up sometimes, and vacationing at the beach every year. Who am I kidding, though, right? Hang on, I'll go change and be right back."

Paula returned in five minutes in sweatpants and a

long-sleeved white Christmas T-shirt with her hair pulled back into a ponytail. "There, the powdered sugar will blend into this shirt better. Ready?"

I bowed and beckoned toward the door to the apartment. "Yep. This way, my lady. The Happy-mobile awaits."

"And Rodney."

"Oh, Monosyllabic Rodney and I had a lengthy conversation this morning."

"You did? And what did you call him?"

"Monosyllabic Rodney. Every time I asked him a question, he answered in one syllable. *Hey, yes, no, fine, okay*—well, that has two, but Rodney's vocabulary is not the broadest. Have you ever wondered why a word meaning *one syllable* has five syllables?"

"You should get out more."

I laughed. "Happy uses it as part of his training with new employees to Happy Electric. Why make things more difficult than necessary? Besides the obvious blessings of the Lord on his business, keeping things simple at every level is one secret of Happy's success."

"Hmm."

"Plus," I whispered as we descended the stairs, "don't you think Monosyllabic Rodney has a friendlier ring to it than Creepy Rodney?"

"Shh, he'll hear you."

THE DRIVE to the New Orleans-style cafe took ten minutes, during which my mind raced, but my mouth remained silent. Paula didn't talk either. I wondered where our conversation would go this morning after we had packed so much into Friday. Except for Lisa's phone call the afternoon before, I would be back in my apartment in Texas, munching on a protein bar, if I had an appetite at all. Instead, I had a date with my wife, though Rodney seemed to be the only person with whom I could call her that without shrinking back from it.

The cafe was bustling with Christmas shoppers preparing for an early start. I ordered beignets for both of us, and we sat at a table next to the front window. An air pot of their signature chickory coffee and a pair of mugs awaited us. No sooner than I had filled out cups, Paula cut to the chase.

"Where do we go from here, Brandon?"

I didn't dare feign ignorance. "Did it hit you that my weekend here is halfway over this morning? It did me. Will you give me a few minutes to walk through my talk with Lisa yesterday? My train of thought will make more sense in context."

Paula flipped her right hand palm up, beckoning me to continue. Before our beignets arrived, I recounted Lisa's revelation and her question about when I fell in love with her mother.

"So what did you tell her?" Paula asked.

"Here you are, two orders of beignets," our server interrupted, sliding a plate of steaming pastries heaped with confectioners' sugar. "Y'all are new here, aren't you? Aren't y'all just the cutest couple? Well, enjoy!" She spun away to return to the kitchen but called back over her shoulder, "Y'all need anything, just holler. My name's Susie."

Something about the way Susie said *holler* caused me to repeat it. "Paula, you need anything? Because I can just holler, and Susie Sunshine will come running. Want me to holler?"

Paula laughed and shook her head at me. "Stop it. You're going to get us in trouble talking about people today."

"Hey, I whispered about Monosyllabic Rodney. And Sunshine Susie? She told us she only responds to hollering. She wasn't much to stick around for answers, was she?"

"No, but I am, and I'm still waiting for you to answer my question."

"Let me ask the blessing first. Since we're such a cute couple, would you mind holding my hand?" Paula extended her hand, and I asked a quick blessing over our food and our day. Before she pushed for my answer again, I shoved a corner of a beignet in my mouth. She took a bite, but her eyes said she was still waiting for a response.

Between my first and second beignets, I repeated the question. "Lisa wanted to know when I first fell in love with you."

"Yes, you said that. What did you tell her?"

"I told her that..." I grabbed another beignet and pushed it in my mouth, scattering powdered sugar all over my face and the front of my sweatshirt. With my mouth full, I mumbled, "Mm, these are delicious. You should eat yours before they get cold."

"The beignets aren't the only things getting cold."

"Okay, fine, but if I have to eat cold beignets, you're bringing me here again." She didn't respond. "I told Lisa that our dating days weren't exactly a courtship like hers and Jake's, but I didn't go so far as to call it a hookup. That sounds so crude, but that's the language you'd use nowadays. I gave her the condensed version of the missing years, most of which she knew from what you shared with your friends on Thanksgiving. I told her about giving my life to the Lord and about Happy, Jacob, and C.J. discipling me and teaching how love should look. She had seen that change firsthand in you, so it made more sense to her than if I had just shared my story."

About that time, Susie bounced over to our table. "How are we doing over here? Everything okay?"

"We're fine, thanks," Paula said, not bothering to look up.

"Super. Well, if y'all need anything..."

"Just holler?" I offered.

"You got it."

I reached for a beignet that had cooled to room temperature. Paula clapped her hand over mine.

"Don't you dare."

"Yes, ma'am. Now, where was I?"

"You know good and well where."

"Okay, I told Lisa I didn't understand what true love was, that I had always been more of a taker than a giver. Paula, do you remember when I picked you up to take you to eat at the fancy steakhouse?"

"That was Thursday. Today is Saturday. Are you still on track?"

"Very much. Do you remember when I asked if it was a date?"

She smiled. "I shouldn't have encouraged you. At the moment, though, I was enjoying the idea of getting dressed up and going out without being the third wheel with Lisa and Jake or Pastor Hobbs and Vicki."

"It was fun for me, too. You threw cold water on our date as soon as we sat down at our table when you started laying out my weekend gauntlet."

"Sorry for getting your hopes up."

"No, that's very much what I expected on the drive east."

"So…?"

"Do you remember what you said after you laid out the hurdles I needed to clear?"

"That I was pulling for you. Something else I should have kept to myself."

"That's when I fell in love with you."

Paula's face fell blank. She fidgeted in her seat, and her hands couldn't find a place to rest. Reaching to swipe her hair still pulled back neatly into her ponytail, she discovered her voice and asked, "Why then in particular?"

"I'm not going to lie—I enjoyed the flirting, and you were the class of the place in Lisa's outfit."

"Hey, I picked out the scarf."

"You did, and what an amazing job you did choosing it. When you marched me through the tests necessary for me to pass to come around again, I recognized *resolve* might not have been just for me. I saw it in you, too. Before, you were my girlfriend and then my wife..."

"Technically, still your wife."

"Yeah, but I identified you from my point of view. You were *my* girlfriend and *my* wife. My understanding of true love from God's perspective, even though it's still elementary, has revealed that I didn't love you like that back then. The closest I came was when you told me you were pregnant with Lisa. Even then, it was about *my* daughter. I didn't love you for who you were. Now, you've lived a tough life, but you've become your own person, not based on who you are to someone else. That classy lady I had dinner with on Thursday night was looking out for herself and her children, but the person she had become allowed hope for me, too. And I realized I loved her."

Someone studying the customers in the café from a distance might have noticed a middle-aged couple sitting next to the window choreographing a new dance. Unable to find a comfortable spot in my chair, I repositioned myself three or four times. Paula continued to swipe at the hair not dangling over her forehead. Susie came by again, and we shook our heads in perfect synchronization. Paula interrupted the dance with an apology.

"Sorry your beignets are cold. We can warm them up in the microwave at my apartment later."

"This was better. I was glad to try my answer out on Lisa first."

"That explains her giddiness last night."

"Yep."

"She can get silly when she's excited about something. I've learned to wait her out, and she'll eventually tell me what's on her mind."

"You have a tell, too."

"What do you mean?"

"I can identify when you want to say something don't know whether you should say it out loud."

"How?"

"You swipe at hair that's not in your eyes."

Paula forced her hands into her lap and ducked her chin into her shirt. "I don't know what you're talking about."

"You have something to say."

"Do not."

"Do."

"Do not."

"What are we, five? How about I help you?"

"I don't need any help."

"Let's say she asked you the same question..."

"Let's say *who* asked me *what*?" Only through supreme concentration did Paula keep her hands in her lap.

I topped off my coffee and let the question hang in the chickory-scented air between us. As I sipped the potent brew that begged for a bite of cold but sweet beignet, I trained my gaze on Paula. Her eyes hinted she was planning her words that would come in her own time. When I reached the bottom of my mug and she still hadn't voiced them, I suggested we ask Sunshine Susie for a carryout box.

"I would tell her the fourth time you left."

I leaned back, leaving her space to explain.

"This weekend, I mean. The first time you walked out without much of an explanation, you went to pick up a car for our baby girl. I thought it odd, but David and I were thinking more about Lisa, so we hoped you were just giving her some space. The second time you left, you kept your word that if any of us said no, you would go back to Texas without a confrontation. As I said Thursday night, I was pulling for you, but I didn't try too hard to talk Lisa back from her response. Like I told you, I had trained my mind to trust Lisa's and David's and Jake's impressions of your intentions more than my own. I was disappointed when you left, but it spoke highly of you that you followed through with your promise.

"The third time you walked out this weekend—during supper last night—was a different story, at least at first. I didn't plan to shame you by retelling the story of the picnic. That hurt me then, and I don't care to go back and dig up old wounds. After so many years, I realized what holding onto my grudges against you—everybody else, too—was doing to me. Only God's grace protected Lisa and David from becoming the bitter person I was, even though I tried not to speak ill of you too much. Anyway, when you insisted I tell the story last night, I was reluctant. Then, when you hopped up and walked out without a word, I felt double crossed. David reached over and put his hand on my arm and told me to let you go, that it would be okay. I trusted him."

Paula broke off, her eyes diverted over my shoulder. I glanced back to see Sunshine Susie approaching our table.

Paula fired first. "We'll holler."

Susie said, "Yes, ma'am" and spun away.

Paula softened after Susie rounded the corner, out of sight. "Better leave her a generous tip."

"Yes, ma'am," I responded, feigning a cat's swipe.

"Stop it. She's getting on my nerves. Can't she tell we're in the middle of an important conversation?"

"Not likely. You were saying…"

"Yeah, I trusted that David understood why you walked out. I thought you had put me in a no-win situation by having me tell the kids about the picnic. And after putting quite an effort into what I considered a meaningful supper."

"It was, especially the habanero sauce. That was a nice touch."

Paula smiled and reached for her forehead, only to yank her hand back into her lap. "When you walked back in carrying two bottles of sparkling grape juice, it was like three things clicked in my brain at one time. First, you noticed what I was cooking and understood what it meant, even though you acted like you didn't. Second, that you set me up by having me tell that story. But third, that you did it because you wanted to redeem it. You entered back into the pain of the past to heal it. I still don't understand a lot about being a Christian, but Pastor Hobbs has worked with me to understand forgiveness, reconciliation, and restoration. They're difficult to live out. And I get what you did, Brandon. Thank you."

"Sounds as though Pastor Hobbs has been your Happy."

"How's that?"

"I think God put Pastor Hobbs and Kerry Hapstead in our paths to teach us what we would need to walk through this. Okay, so if my math is right, you're missing a fourth time when I've walked out this week-end. I'm only counting three."

"Remember the original question?"

"What you would tell Lisa if she asked when you fell in love with me."

"When you and Jake left for his apartment last night, I missed you as soon as you walked out the door. That's what I would tell her. I would love to say that's when I realized I *still* loved you, but I'm not sure I ever did back then. I'm sorry if that hurts your feelings, but you weren't very lovable back then. But neither was I."

"Not true. I just wasn't capable. So… where does that leave us now?"

"Another leg of the gauntlet."

"Oh, boy. What is it?"

"Change of plans for lunch today. You and I will dine with my parents."

"Bring it on."

A FEW MINUTES LATER, Paula and I sat in my truck and watched through the front window of the café as a white-aproned server picked up a folded napkin. She read the words *Merry Christmas* in a woman's handwriting. The *C* was decorated with rays of sunshine and a smiley face. She unfolded the napkin and tucked the two twenty-dollar bills into her apron. Mr. Doris would have loved to see it. I reached between the seats and searched for her card, to no avail. I determined to find it after I dropped Paula off at her apartment to change out of her sugarcoated shirt.

25

I ended up on my back searching for Ms. Doris's card between the seats on my truck parked at Jake's apartment complex. The white card was stuck halfway to the floorboard. I pulled it and read it again before calling. *Doris Clausen. Call me if you need me.* I wondered how many people ever used the card to inform her how God had answered her prayers for them. I tapped the digits. After four rings, her voice mail message greeted me.

"Hello, dear, this is Doris. If you're calling this number, you need me to pray for you. I can't come to the phone because I'm at work or church. If you'll leave me a message, I promise I'll pray for you as soon as I listen to it. If you'd rather I call you back, I'd be happy to do that, too. But listen, dear, you don't need me as much as you think. God is ready to hear from you. Just call out to Him in your own words. I hope you'll do that. Thank you, dear. Have a blessed day."

I ended the call after listening to the message, but called right back and left a message. "Hey, Ms. Doris, this is Brandon Wade. You prayed for me twice this weekend about being restored to my family. I just wanted to call and let you know God is answering your prayers—and many others—more powerfully than I could have imagined. I'll try to catch you at a better time and tell you all about it. If I ever drive through Clinton again on any day but Sunday, I'll drop by to see you. Thanks again for your prayers. Goodbye, Ms. Doris."

"READY?"

"No. What am I supposed to say to your parents that I should have met over twenty years ago."

"Just be yourself—the new you."

"What are your parents like?"

"Crusty and sweet. Dad retired so he could rid his yard of varmints he'll describe in detail. Be sure to compliment him on whatever landscaping project he's working on this weekend. Mom will be in the kitchen baking for a neighbor because homemade is better than store-bought. She keeps their cul-de-sac supplied with cakes and pies and cookies. As you might imagine, the neighbors love her."

"I don't possess much expertise in varmint control, but I like cake," I quipped.

"Oh, and one more thing," Paula added with a wink before she ducked into my truck.

"And that is?"

"They don't know you're here."

"You didn't tell them?"

"None of this, not even my trip to see you in Texas. They thought I was driving out there to visit a friend. Mom and Dad were so glad to discover I had a friend that they didn't ask many questions. I offered nothing after I returned except that my friend and I had a pleasant visit. Mom was disappointed she hadn't sent a loaf of homemade bread."

"That is disappointing."

"I didn't intend on breaking bread with you, if you'll recall."

"I'm lucky you didn't break something else."

"Blessed."

"Huh?"

"Not lucky. Blessed."

"Right. How do you plan to introduce me?"

"What do you mean?"

"Well, I could be the vagabond ex-husband who is not *ex* at all, or I could be your 'friend' you're involved enough with to bring over to meet them."

"Don't you think they'll be suspicious when I introduce you as *Brandon*?"

"Maybe you have a type. It's a common enough name. Plus, I don't fit the description they have of me."

"I don't believe deception is the most direct path to their hearts."

"You're right. Just an idea. Chalk it up to nerves. A dude in his mid-forties shouldn't be nervous about meeting his wife's parents."

"I wouldn't describe anything about our relationship as normal—then or now, would you?"

"No." Paula was so at odds with her parents in our early years together that she neglected to mention me. I didn't encourage her in that direction, either. After I left, she felt guilty about keeping them from their grandchildren, so she moved toward restoration with her mom and dad. She had showed me where they lived once, but that was as close as I had come to meeting them.

"Up here." Paula pointed to a modest red brick house on the right side of a short cul-de-sac of six houses. Outside, a man I assumed to be her father stood with one hand on his hip and another on the handle of a garden rake, contemplating an empty flowerbed full of leaves. He was wearing a red flannel shirt and gray sweatpants that gathered at the bottom to reveal his argyle socks that dove into his brown dress shoes.

"Don't judge," Paula admonished. "He's my daddy, and I love him, even though he doesn't have a lick of fashion sense."

I turned the truck into the driveway. Paula's dad didn't turn to look, even as we walked across the yard toward him, more focused on his work.

Without a word of introduction or other acknowledgment of our presence, he said, "I'm figuring out whether I should clear the leaves out of the flowerbed or just mulch over them next spring. They'll provide nutrients to the soil if I leave them, but they'll be butt ugly all winter." He turned to us without surprise and looked directly at me. "What do you think?"

"Well… uh… since the leaves have all fallen from the trees, could you mulch over them now?"

He considered my suggestion for a moment. "Hmm, two birds with one stone. Where have you been keeping this one, Paula?"

"Daddy, this is Brandon. Brandon, this is my daddy."

"My name's Jerry," he said, removing his right gardening glove and offering his hand. "Brandon, huh? I reckon she's told you about her loser first husband with the same name?"

He returned his gaze to the flowerbed, imagining the leaves covered with a layer of fresh mulch. I winked at Paula before responding, "Yeah, I know all about him."

"You showed him to you mama?"

"No, Daddy, we just got here. I'll take him inside now."

"Tell her I'll be on in a minute."

"Yes, sir."

As we turned to walk toward the house, I caught a sudden movement at the front window, where Paula's mother had been watching us. We walked up the manicured front walkway toward the door, where the aroma of fresh bread greeted us as soon as Paula pushed the door open. Her mother scurried from the kitchen, posing as surprised we had arrived.

"Mama, this is Brandon. Brandon, this is my mom."

"Call me Phyllis," her mother said, rushing to take my hand for a more proper greeting. "Y'all come on in and sit down. I just took a fresh-baked loaf of homemade bread out of the oven. You like homemade bread, don't you, Brandon?"

"Oh, yes, ma'am. It smells delicious."

Pleased, Phyllis changed gears. "Paula, will you tell your father to come in and get cleaned up for supper?"

"He said he'd be here in a minute."

"He always says that. His *minutes* never last sixty seconds. So, Brandon, did Paula tell you about her first husband?"

"He knows all about him," Jerry growled, appearing behind Phyllis. "Boy can't help his name. Leave him alone."

"I'm sorry. Get cleaned up, dear, and let's eat."

"What do you think I'm doing?"

"Well, you don't have to be ugly about it."

"THIS IS HOMEMADE SOURDOUGH BREAD," Phyllis announced. "Do you like it, Brandon?"

"Yes, ma'am, very much," I answered.

"I make fresh bread at least once a week."

Jerry growled, "She thinks it's her responsibility to feed everyone in the neighborhood."

Phyllis turned to face me, ignoring her husband, which seemed second nature to her. "The neighbors seem to appreciate my culinary efforts more than Jerry does. Most of the time, I don't make it to their doors before they meet me on the porch. I receive invitations to chat on front porches in the neighborhood all the time while Jerry stays here and guards his fortress."

"If I left it up to you, the school kids would tramp out a path across our yard," Jerry snapped.

"We have five children in the neighborhood who ride the school bus," Phyllis explained, again directly to me. "The bus driver drops them off at the corner, and they could save a few steps crossing our yard on their walks home after a long day at school. Jerry takes his lawn chair down to the corner to scare the kids off his precious lawn."

"It works, doesn't it?"

Phyllis never peeled her gaze from me, maintaining a pleasant countenance. "Brandon, you might have noticed a faint path across the yard. That's from Jerry walking the same route to the corner to keep those poor kids from making a path across the yard. So you're enjoying the bread?"

I nodded and stuffed the last corner into my mouth to stifle a chuckle at her deft return to her topic of choice. Before I finished chewing, she offered another slice, cutting it and placing it on my plate without giving me a chance to respond. I complimented every item on the table, from the edible to the decorative. Paula ducked her head to stifle a grin every time I did so.

"Real unfortunate name you got there, Brandon," Jerry inserted after Phyllis had excluded him from the conversation too long for his liking. "Paula's first husband's name was Brandon, too. Real loser, that guy. She's told you all about him, I reckon."

"You didn't like him much, huh?" I asked. Paula backhanded my leg under the table.

"Heavens, no. He ran off on her, you know."

"So Paula says. Tell me about him."

"Never met the guy. Paula never brought him around to introduce him to her parents. We could have steered her clear of him, that's for sure."

"Wait, she married this fellow without ever bringing him by to meet her parents? What kind of man does that?" I felt another pop under the table.

"You're spot on, there, boy." Jerry pointed his fork at me while finishing a bite of fried chicken. "I'm a fair judge of character, and I could have warned her to steer clear of him, but she wanted nothing to do with us."

"Rebellious child, huh?" Paula pinched my leg this time.

Jerry rocked back in his chair, roaring with laughter. "You talk like you knew her back then. Let me tell you, this one…" He shifted his pointer fork to Paula. "She was a piece of work then."

"What about now?"

"Aw, I reckon she's straightened up since having kids of her own."

"This other Brandon—is he still around?"

Paula coughed her way through a laugh she couldn't contain. Phyllis checked on her when she turned red, but Paula waved her off and claimed some sweet tea just went down the wrong side.

"Naw," Jerry continued, "that boy lit a shuck for Texas, I believe it was. We ain't seen hide nor hair of him for better than twenty years. Where are you from, son?"

"Born and raised right here in Harriston."

"That a fact?"

"Yes, sir."

"What kind of work do you do?"

"Electrical."

"Master electrician?"

"No, sir, working through apprentice school."

Jerry cocked his head to the side. "Kinda old for apprentice school, ain't you?"

"Oldest in my class. I met a guy I wanted to work for and started working my way up from the bottom. He mentors me while I work my way up in the company."

"Humph. What's the name of this outfit?"

"Happy Electric Company."

"Happy Electric, huh? Never heard of them. With all the construction west of town, fly-by-night companies keep popping up all the time. I wouldn't hire anybody but Stapleford Construction. They do a little of everything. Been in business since I was a boy. The owner died last year, I believe it was, and his boys are running it now. They'll probably run it in the ground."

"Mr. Sunshine and Roses," Phyllis mumbled under her breath.

"Stapleford?" I asked, turning to Paula. "Where have I heard that name before?"

"Vicki Stapleford. You met her at the Turners' Thursday night. The owner was her husband. I'm going to work for the company on Monday before they run it in the ground."

"Roger Stapleford, that was his name," Jerry growled. "Word is she's taken up with a pastor fellow already and Roger not dead a year yet."

"Watch it, Daddy. That's my pastor you're talking

about, and I guarantee there has been nothing less than honorable about their relationship. Move along." I scooped a bite of lukewarm mashed potatoes to camouflage a grin for Paula's spunk.

"What were we talking about?" Jerry asked himself.

"Putting somebody down, I'm sure," Phyllis mumbled.

Jerry ignored her. "Happy Electric, that's what we were talking about. Now, Brandon, if I was you…"

"And you're not," Phyllis said, louder this time.

"Like I said, if I was you, I'd at least turn in an application over at Stapleford. You never know about these here-today-gone-tomorrow companies. Who knows, they might hire you one day."

"Yes, sir. That's a good idea."

"What's the deal with the smiley-face logo on the side of your truck? What genius came up with that?"

Paula endured another coughing fit, but I kept a straight face. "Owner of the company. His name is Kerry Hapstead, but everybody calls him Happy."

"Unfortunate for him."

"Says Grumpy," Phyllis added.

"Oh, mind your own beeswax."

"Nobody says that anymore, dear."

"I don't care what everybody else says. So, Brandon, what size outfit is this Happy Electric?"

"Around thirty crews, about half commercial and half residential. We've added five crews this year and should add at least that many next year."

"That's sizable for me to have never heard of Happy Electric. Where do you work, mostly?"

"Dallas."

"Dallas? You mean, like in Texas?"

"Yes, sir." As I confirmed Dallas's location in Texas, my phoned buzzed with a call from Doris Clausen.

"I thought you were from Harriston."

"I am. I've been working in Texas for a while. Y'all, please excuse me. I have a call that I must answer." I slipped away from the table and rushed out the front door to accept the call.

26

"Ms. Doris?"

"No, this is Glen Clausen, Doris's son."

"Oh?"

"Is this Brandon?"

"Yes."

"Brandon, I'm returning calls from the messages in Mama's voice mail."

"Is everything okay?"

"Mama's been eaten up with cancer for a long time, Brandon. I don't know if she told you that—she didn't make my sisters and me aware of it until Friday. She dropped by my house on her way home from work and told me about her day. She stood up to leave and told me about her cancer, like she was telling me what she was having for dinner. I called my sisters, and we drove over to see her this afternoon to find out what was going on—they didn't have a clue, either. She didn't answer the door, so I used my key to get in, and we found her in the bed. She had the biggest smile on her face, and I asked her what she was so happy about. When she didn't answer, I asked again, and she still didn't respond. That's when I realized she wasn't moving. She was gone."

"Oh, my gosh. She's…?"

"Dead. Happy as a lark about something, but she was gone."

I collapsed on the top step of the porch. "Glen, I'm… I'm so sorry. I don't know what to say."

"Not much to say. She has lived by herself since Daddy died five years ago. Wouldn't hear of moving in with any of her kids. Loved her job, though we thought it was because it gave her something to do. I imagine you are evidence it was more than that. She left a note beside her bed, along with a phone we didn't realize she had—a second phone. The note instructed us to answer her messages right away. My sisters were too torn up to do it, so it fell to me. You're the fourth call I've returned."

"I can't believe…"

"Yeah, you wouldn't recognize anything was wrong with her. She stopped by my house two or three times a week, so I should have noticed before anybody else. She looked worn out on Friday, but that's not unusual after one of her shifts. They should have known better than to have worked a woman her age that hard." He paused for a moment. "I'm sorry to ramble on, but it still hasn't set in that she's gone and that she kept so much a secret from us. Brandon, what's your connection to Mama?"

"Glen, if I had to guess, I'm the reason your mother

seemed worn out after work on Friday."

"You—why?"

Without considering my rudeness to Paula's parents for staying outside so long, I filled Glen in on my two interactions with Ms. Doris.

"So this number was some sort of prayer hotline?"

"It appears so." I described the card she had handed me. "I figured I wasn't the only one she spotted carrying the weight of the world on his shoulders at her job. She was a people watcher, for sure. When God answered her prayers so specifically, I figured it would encourage her to hear my story since. I doubt many folks took time to thank her for the other side of her prayers. Several times earlier, I planned to call, but her card fell between the seats of my truck, and it kept slipping my mind to search for it until this afternoon. I had no idea she…"

After another long pause, Glen said, "Brandon, yours was the last message on her voicemail. There were no new messages, so I believe she listened to your story. It may have been the last thing she heard before she…" His voice wobbled, the first time it had done so during our conversation. "I think your message is the reason we found Mama with such a radiant smile on her face."

I had no words to say in response, but I broke down and cried on Paula's parents' front steps. After I found enough composure to tell Glen I was sorry for his loss again and tell him goodbye, I pulled the phone away from my ear. Before I could end the call, I heard him calling my name again. "Yes?"

"I wonder if it might be all right if we played your message at Mama's funeral."

"Oh, my goodness, yes."

"We're still piecing together the parts of her life that we weren't aware of, but evidently, she blessed quite a few people. I imagine she would want that represented at her service."

"Glen, I want to ask you a question," I said, emboldened with a power I had not felt before during our call.

"Shoot."

"Do you have a personal relationship with Jesus like your mama did?"

Glen didn't answer for quite a while. I wondered if we had lost our connection before he responded. "I walked the aisle at church when I was twelve, but I guess I've gone my own way since then and done things I'm not proud to share. Seems I have some soul searching to do."

"Don't take too long. Glen, I'm sitting on the front steps of my in-laws' house right now. My wife that I abandoned twenty years ago all but told me she loved me today, and we're several steps down the path toward reconciling with one another. What's happening to us is unheard of, except in God's story. It took both of us coming to Jesus, and it took some well-timed encouragement from your precious mother, but if God can redeem my sorry life, you're not too far gone. I promise, Glen, God will accept you if you run to Him."

"Thanks. I'll think about it."

"Look, you have my number. If I can pray for you like your mother did for me, you don't hesitate to call."

"Thanks, I will."

"And, Glen?"

"Yeah?"

"Thanks for calling. I am so sorry for your loss, but your mother was a remarkable woman that God used at one of the most fragile moments in my journey with Him. I can't even imagine her joy at being with Jesus right now."

Glen laughed, a half-chuckle. "If you had seen her face this afternoon, you could."

We said goodbye, and after making sure he ended the call first, I mounted the steps to go explain my extended absence from the dinner table. I wiped my eyes with my sleeve and walked back through the front door.

I SENSED the dynamic of the room had changed when I returned inside. Jerry glared at me, and Phyllis shifted in her chair. Paula asked, "Is everything okay?"

"Not really," I sniffed. "That call was to tell me a dear friend of mine passed away today."

"Oh, I'm sorry," Phyllis offered.

"How old a fella was he?" Jerry asked, more gruffly than sympathetically.

"She."

"She? You make a practice of buddying up with girls?"

"Jerry!" Phyllis scolded.

"No," I said, ignoring his crudeness. "She was much older than me, but we had a special relationship."

"Special enough for you to run off to Texas with

her?"

I glanced at Paula.

"I told them."

"Did you also inform them…?"

"I told them everything, including the last three days."

"Then let me tell you my history with Ms. Doris." I had not informed Paula of my stops in Clinton and my chats with my prayer champion. After had I caught her and her parents up to speed, I shared my conversation with Glen.

Paula's hand found mine under the table. She squeezed it and released. "I'm sorry about your friend," she whispered. "We can go whenever you're ready."

Jerry turned toward me with a hint of aggression, apparently considering my grieving period for Ms. Doris complete. "So, you're the Brandon who left our girl to raise two kids by herself?"

"Yes, sir, that's me. I'm not the same person I was then, but I understand if you don't appreciate my being here. You may not be ready to have this conversation, but I would appreciate the opportunity to ask your forgiveness for bailing on your daughter and grandchildren."

"It's them you need to ask," Jerry barked.

"He has, Daddy, and we've forgiven him."

"Doesn't mean you have to bring him around. You should send his scrawny butt behind to Texas."

"Daddy, he's sitting right here. If you have something to say…"

"You know what, I believe I've had enough of this

charade. You want to keep him around, that's your business, but I don't have to sit here and act like nothing ever happened. I'm going out back to my shed to clean my tools. Phyllis, you can call me when the both of them are out of my house." He stormed out, slamming the back door behind him for emphasis.

Phyllis studied my reaction. "Don't mind my husband, Brandon. If you prove yourself with Paula and our grandchildren, he'll come around in another twenty, thirty years. Tell me, what are your intentions?"

"Ms. Phyllis, I came this weekend to say I'm sorry and ask forgiveness from Lisa and David. I came with hopes but not expectations. My intentions are not to make anybody mad or uncomfortable. I'm taking my lead on next steps from Paula, Lisa, and David. With their blessing, I plan to be here for Lisa's graduation and wedding. We haven't had any discussions past that."

"Well, nobody asked me, but I think you all are moving too fast. That's my two cents, but you and Paula are adults who can make your own decisions." With that, she gathered her dishes and marched into the kitchen and didn't return.

"Let's go," Paula said.

I thought she was premature to give up. "Just like that?"

"We'll come back another time. Neither of them are likely to change their mind tonight. Let them be."

"If you say so."

"I say so."

THE REST of the weekend unwound faster than I could grasp the moments. After church on Sunday morning, lunch with Paula, Lisa, David, and Jake flew by. My time in Mississippi had ticked by much too fast. I ran by Jake's after lunch to brush my teeth and grab my duffel bag, while dreading the goodbyes waiting for me at Paula's apartment. I reminded myself of my word for the week, *resolve,* and drove over to bid what I hoped to be temporary farewells.

No one was sitting when I entered the apartment. I made my way around the room, intent on keeping my composure.

"Jake, it was so nice to meet you. Lisa chose well."

"Thank you, sir. You'll be back for our wedding?"

"Count on it."

"You can plan on staying at my place again."

"Thanks. I appreciate the offer. You were a great host, but you'll be getting a much better roommate soon."

Lisa smiled and stretched both of her arms around my neck. "See you in three weeks." When she pulled me close, she whispered, "I love you, Daddy. Thank you for coming back."

I whispered back, "Thank you for giving me another chance. You're going to be a beautiful bride. I'll see you then. I love you, too."

"David," I said, making my way around the semicircle and reaching for his firm hand, "I can't tell you how proud I am of you. You're ten times the man I ever thought about being."

"I don't know about all that," he said, "but I've

missed you all these years. Thank you for facing the gauntlet this weekend to make things right with us."

"It's a step."

"A big one. Stay in touch. I'll see you in three weeks."

When I reached Paula, I held out my hands for hers. Instead of taking both of them, she took my right hand and pulled me toward the door. I waved farewell to the kids and closed the door behind us.

"You need to get on the road," Paula started. "Let's give this weekend a few days to settle in and then see how we feel."

"Okay." Her brusque sendoff was disappointing after our moments of near romance over the past three days. It was for the best, I convinced myself. If she had hope for a relationship in our future like I did, God would work out the timing. "Paula, thanks for everything. We saw a lot of answered prayers, didn't we?"

Her weak smile convinced me she didn't want to see me go, so I determined to make our goodbye quick and painless. I reached for her, and she melted into my arms, but only for three or four seconds. She pulled back, locking eyes with me for the briefest of moments. "You'd better get going. Let me know when you get home."

"Count on it."

"I will."

I took the first long step toward the stairs and picked up the pace as I walked away. Turning the corner to descend the steps, I blinked back tears, determined to put up a brave front until I drove out of Paula's sight. I reached the bottom and turned toward my truck, looking back and almost bumping into one of Paula's neighbors.

"Rodney."

"Brandon."

A minute later, pulling my key from my pocket, I allowed myself a glance upstairs. Paula still stood alone in front of her door, holding her face in her hands. I pulled the door open, looked back upstairs, and spotted Paula dabbing her eyes. Throwing the key on the seat, I spun around and marched back toward the stairs.

"Forget something?" Rodney asked, his flurry of syllables surprising me.

"Yeah, Rodney, I forgot something very important."

Paula met me halfway once I reached the top of the stairs and fell into my arms. "I don't want you to go."

"Paula," I said, pushing her shoulders away from me so I could lock eyes with her. "At the cafe Saturday morning, I all but said something I need to tell you before I drive away. I love you."

Her face broke. "I wanted to tell you, but you needed to say it first. I love you, too. Pray hard, Brandon. I want to make this work. "

"Count on it."

"I will."

I reached for my wife one more time and kissed her on the lips. I wanted to kiss her again and again, but I resisted. Instead, I hoped my eyes conveyed my commitment to see God's miracle through whatever obstacles remained. And then I walked to my truck and drove back to Texas.

27

The setting for the wedding was perfect. An outdoor wedding in December can be a risky undertaking, even in the South. As unpretentious as the wedding party was, a move indoors on short notice would not have been the ordeal of a larger wedding party, but the weather on this day was ideal. The wedding venue smelled of Christmas, with fresh greenery all around.

Pastor Hobbs stood in front with the groom, just days shy of his own wedding with Vicki. The rest of Paula's Lonesome, party of six crew and their guests milled around the venue. Easton Sterling and Sherrill Riggs would later man a table, serving a small but nifty groom's cake with lemon curd filling and vanilla butter-cream—or so Lisa had informed me. Irv and Carol Turner prepared to serve the bride's cake, a larger but still budget-conscious three-tiered naked strawberry cake adorned with chocolate-covered strawberries.

Paula had described it to me, and I looked forward to sinking my teeth into a piece since I hadn't felt like eating all day.

Tara Cates straightened her little boy's collar before he walked down the aisle as the ring bearer. Austen Thomason snapped photo after photo of the two of them and everyone else in attendance. After greeting guests and encouraging them to sign the guest book, Mr. Jimmy Lee Yates found his seat near the front on the groom's side, where more empty seats remained.

Though the bride and groom had designed the wedding as a casual affair, Paula looked stunning as she walked down the small center aisle to join me. Lisa had called her dress a silver sheath style with poet sleeves. That meant little to me, but she was gorgeous in it, and that my daughter's working capacity amazed me. Even while juggling finals, graduation, and wedding preparation, Lisa had taken Paula shopping for the better part of a Saturday to find the perfect dress for the wedding.

I had shown a photo of Paula's dress—Lisa said I would have to wait until the wedding to see her wearing it—to Happy one day after work. He had insisted I wear new clothes to match. He had Emily, my boss, send me to a location where we didn't have a crew one day, a high-end men's clothing store. Happy was waiting for me there with strict instructions to ignore every price tag. Two hours later, I walked out with gray denim trousers, a silver dress shirt, black vest, and black dress boots. Still, as Paula neared my spot, I had clearly outkicked my coverage, as Happy often said of his wife.

The sun was dipping near the tree line in the western

sky when the wedding party Pastor Hobbs began the ceremony. I couldn't help but notice how satisfied Lisa and Jake appeared together. Both of them smiled broadly as Pastor Hobbs cleared his throat to speak.

"DEARLY BELOVED, we have come together in God's presense to witness and bless the joining of this man and this woman in holy matrimony. God established the bond and covenant of marriage in creation, and our Lord Jesus Christ affirmed this manner of life by His presence and first miracle at a wedding. It signifies to us the mystery of the union between Christ and His Church, and Holy Scripture commends it to be honored among all people.

"God intended the union of husband and wife for their mutual joy, help, and comfort during prosperity and adversity. Therefore, marriage is not to be entered into lightly, but with reverence in accordance with the purposes for which God instituted it. I have counseled this couple and believe them to be ready to represent Christ through their union as husband and wife."

Pastor Hobbs asked for any objections, and no one voiced any. My attention strayed for a moment as I wondered if anyone ever had. Perhaps someone should have objected to Paula's and my wedding so many years ago. Her father would have. Our marriage seemed like an alternate universe in so many ways, but Lisa and David were living proof that it existed.

I snapped back to the present as Pastor Hobbs asked

the glowing bride if she would "have this man to be your husband and to live together with him in covenant marriage." He asked if she would "love him, comfort him, honor and keep him, in sickness and in health; and, forsaking all others, be faithful unto him as long as you both shall live." She assented, as he had a few moments earlier.

Pastor Hobbs asked the audience if they would "uphold these two persons in their marriage." As they eagerly offered their agreement, I considered how different Christian vows were than the ones I didn't even recall from the justice of the peace who had married Paula and me. I blinked hard twice to jerk myself back to the reality of the moment, where Pastor Hobbs inquired, "Who gives this woman to be married to this man?"

David stood straight as he responded, "She gives herself of her own accord, with her family's blessing." I'm sure Paula's pride in our son surpassed my own from her greater investment in him, but my smile matched hers on this day. He and Lisa had worked on his answer to the pastor's question until they were happy with it. Neither my family nor Paula's dad attended our wedding. I wished my parents had lived to see this one. I wasn't able to ask their forgiveness for my rebellion before they died in a car accident months after I hooked up with Paula. When Paula's dad had refused to attend a wedding at which I would be present, she conferred with David, Lisa, and Jake. They agreed to proceed without him. Paula's mom sat proudly on the bride's side, not about to miss this celebration.

After David took his seat, I snapped back to attention as Pastor Hobbs read the groom's vows. Again, I noted promises I had not kept for the past twenty years regarding better and worse, richer and poorer, and sickness and health. I noted the vows began with "in the name of God," whom I had not known when I exchanged words with Paula, and ended with, "This is my solemn vow." The depth of the wedding vows struck me deep in my soul and steeled my determination to make good on over twenty years of failure as a husband.

As the bride repeated her vows, I peeked over my right shoulder as the afternoon sun dipped into a gap among the pines. The entire setting struck me as surreal, and I whispered a prayer thanking God for the kindness of a stranger that changed the course of Paula's life. Her releasing her bitterness toward me led to her driving to Texas to make things right with me. Now, here I was in this beautiful venue, celebrating the wonder of marriage with my family. My eyes moistened when I caught a glance of Austen snapping pictures of little Zan as he approached the wedding party with the rings.

Pastor Hobbs prayed over the rings as a symbol of the vows of the bride and groom before they exchanged rings. Both repeated, "I give you this ring as a symbol of my love, and with all that I am, and all that I have, I honor you, in the name of the Father and the Son and the Holy Spirit." When the rings nestled on their appropriate fingers, Pastor Hobbs pronounced the bride and groom husband and wife in the name of the Father and the Son and the Holy Spirit. Then, he did something I would have never dreamed of doing twenty years earlier, asking the groom to pray over his new bride. I would bet my last dollar that the justice of the peace who married Paula and me had never included something like that in the weddings he had officiated.

After the groom concluded his prayer, Pastor Hobbs announced, "Those whom God has joined together, let no one put asunder." To the bride and groom, he said, "Having witnessed your vows of love to one another, it is my joy to present you to all gathered here as husband and wife. Brandon, you may kiss your bride."

With the sun nestled in the gap between the pines and its reflection lighting up Happy's lake, I kissed my bride. With gusto.

"Ladies and gentlemen," Pastor Hobbs announced, "I present to you Mr. and Mrs. Brandon Wade!"

"I LIKE MY NEW NAME," Paula said, staring out the window at the clouds rising to meet her. "I won't have to spell it or explain it anymore."

"New me, new us," I said as I leaned over her shoulder to see Dallas shrinking below us. "I still can't believe it's real."

"Me either. I can't believe how much Happy spent on bringing everybody out to his place."

"God showed this to him before either of us dreamed it. During these last few months when God has been drawing us to one another, Happy has been cheering us on from several steps ahead. He insisted."

"What will he do without you?"

"I can assure you I needed Kerry Hapstead worse than he needed me. He will find the next Brandon Wade and bring him along soon enough."

"His place was so beautiful. I'm looking forward to spending some time with the Lord there. And learning to fish."

"Huh?"

"He made me promise we would come out and spend some time with him and his wife next summer. I figured it was okay to make that commitment for the both of us."

"The timing this weekend was perfect."

"I know, right? Lisa and Jake just back from their honeymoon. And we'll be home from ours in the nick of time to go to Pastor Hobbs' and Vicki's wedding."

"Boss lady."

"You shouldn't call her that."

"I won't, but I'm happy to have work waiting on me after the first of the year."

"With me. Did you know our son wrote me a check for a week's pay as soon as I told him our plans and wouldn't take any fussing over it?"

"Speaking of our son, have you noticed how his eyes twinkle when he's around a certain photographer?"

Paula turned from the window, the ground below us having disappeared from view. "I have. He won't hear of asking her out, though. He says there's too much difference in their ages. She's only two or three years older than him, which I told him wouldn't matter much when they get a little older, but he's twenty-one and has his mind made up. Let's not push him. If God means for them to be together, it'll happen."

"We're proof of that. They'll have plenty of other occasions to bump into one another over the next few months, it appears."

"Yeah, starting next week at Pastor Hobbs' wedding and then at Irv and Carol's daughters' double wedding."

"What about Easton and Sherrill? I can't see them waiting much longer."

"Well, they've only been dating for a month, but…"

"What?"

"Can you keep a secret?"

"I kept you a secret from most people I worked with in Texas."

"Touché. Easton showed me the ring he plans to put on Sherrill's finger this spring. He wants to marry her after baseball season, so keep your weekends free. We'll get to sample some Memphis barbecue."

"I'm down with that. No way we can match his wedding gift to us, though. This trip was beyond generous."

"I told him the same thing. When my Lonesome crew met, though, we were each the kind of lonely only God can fix. And He did. Easton and I became sandpaper to one other as we told our stories. I pushed him to say aloud obvious things that everybody else noticed, and he did the same for me. One of the deepest roots of bitterness for me was the beach trip you never quite delivered. When you returned to Texas after meeting my Lonesome crew, I talked to each of them to confirm what

I was feeling. I saved Easton for last because more than any of the rest of them, he would tell me the truth if he had any reservations."

"Did he?"

"No, but when I told him our relationship had taken some major steps over the weekend, he cautioned me to slow down and give you time to prove yourself. If you remember his story, you see the irony in his telling anyone to take it slow. His opinion changed, though, when I told him about your walking back in with the sparkling grape juice to our dinner. He understood the significance of your reaching into the past to redeem that night. He shut up then, other than to wish us well. When you told me he had reached out to you to give us a tropical honeymoon, it clicked that he wanted to help you redeem that deepest hurt."

"If we're ever rich like him, we'll do stuff like that, okay?"

"We don't have to be rich like Easton."

"What do you mean?"

"Remember where this started?"

"Where?"

"Austen paid for six meals that cost her maybe a hundred-and-fifty bucks, tip included."

"Right. Got it."

"WOULD YOU LIKE SOMETHING TO DRINK?" the flight attendant asked.

"Something tropical," I replied. "Let's have two orange juices."

"You two look happy," the otherwise disinterested attendant noticed. As she reached for cups with one hand and orange juice with the other, she asked, "Are you…"

"Anniversary trip," I replied at the same time Paula said, "Honeymoon."

Our wide smiles answered her scrunched brows. "We remarried. It's a long story, an unbelievable one."

She mumbled a reply I didn't hear or ask her to repeat. When she moved her cart down the aisle, though, a woman sitting on the other side of the aisle sat staring at us. "That was rude of her. I would love to hear your story."

Paula and I have been telling the story of God's restoration of our marriage ever since.

www.ingramcontent.com/pod-product-compliance
Lightning Source LLC
LaVergne TN
LVHW091118080826
845145LV00008B/1960
* 9 7 8 1 7 3 5 8 0 6 5 3 2 *